FROM THIS MOMENT ON

Windswept Bay, Book One

DEBRA
CLOPTON

CHAPTER ONE

Turbulence rattled the plane and Grant Ellington's nerves at the same time. Digging his fingers into the armrest, he stared out the window and focused on the topaz water below as he struggled to ignore the pounding of his heart. A tall order considering this was his first flight after living through a plane crash six months ago. A crash that he'd lived through and two men hadn't. Two good men.

Grant leaned his head back and closed his eyes. His heart ached. He'd lost his best friend, David, that day and the young wife of the charter pilot lost her husband.

Both men had been good men and they'd perished while Grant had walked away with barely a scratch.

It was hard for him to understand. Hard for him to know why he'd lived and they hadn't.

The rough-riding 747 dipped. Grant's mouth went dry as the memory of lightning striking the small charter plane on its final approach erupted in a flashback…something he hadn't overcome yet and wasn't sure he ever would.

Six endless months and he was still numb and dazed by the loss of the other two men. Their deaths clung to him every moment of the day and most sleepless nights.

Suddenly, the giant 747 lurched violently and his heart slammed into his ribs. "Give me a break," he muttered. He stared out the first class window as the plane crossed from the blue water to flying over land as icy fingers seemed to claw at his insides. "Where's the *blasted* runway?" he growled.

"It'll be okay, dear."

The soft, crackly Southern drawl startled him and he looked to find the tiny, older lady in the seat next to him awake and smiling gently. She'd been snoring peacefully in her seat for the entire trip. Now, she laid a fragile hand on his wrist and patted warm fingers against his clammy skin. He blinked at her, certain he looked like a deer in headlights. He willed his heart to stop racing, willed the panic attack to go away. Wished belatedly that he'd bought the ticket to the seat beside him so there would have been no witness to his breakdown.

But no, she watched him with kind eyes—or more than likely, pity-filled eyes.

He hated pity.

It was especially humiliating considering her snoring had been indication enough that she wasn't in the least bit worried about the flight.

She tapped her fingertips to his damp skin. "You're sweating like a water sprinkler. I have a sister who has a fear of flying. She does the same thing. Wringing wet like a dishrag when we finally stop."

He related to the other woman enduring the ride while sitting beside her cool-as-a-cucumber sister. He rubbed the furrows between his eyes. It didn't matter that he'd lived through disaster; it was still demoralizing that she knew he was terrified.

She leaned closer; the faint scent of gardenias wafted his way. "I don't mind the flight myself, but I've always hated the landings so don't feel bad," she said, as if reading his mind. "However, I say my prayers every time the captain tells us to prepare for landing and then I leave it to God. It works *wonders* for your nerves."

Grant's eyes narrowed. He didn't point out that she'd snored straight through the captain's announcement to prepare for landing so her prayers hadn't been said this trip. The plane shuddered and instantly her startlingly, firm hand grasped his forearm and squeezed. His gaze locked onto hers.

She smiled and then smoothed her hand over Grant's taut muscle. "I don't mind saying that it makes me feel better knowing that a big, strapping man such as yourself can be terrified of landings too." She blinked innocently behind her glasses. "It'll make my sister feel better too."

"Thanks." *I guess*. He grimaced a smile and told

himself she'd been trying to make him feel better, *not* make him feel worse than he had five minutes ago.

"Oh, it was *my* pleasure." Her hand moved to his bicep and her eyes widened. "These arms of yours are hard as petrified timber," she drawled, making the word sound more like *timba.* "Do you do a lot of ranch work?"

How did she know he ranched? "Some," he managed over the lump, glad he sounded halfway normal. Truth was he owned a small ranch but leased his grazing land to his neighbor Cam Sinclair, allowing Cam's cattle to graze on Grant's land. The arrangement worked out well for both of them because he was too busy with his art and traveling to raise cattle and tend to his land himself. At least, he had been too busy traveling prior to the crash. He hadn't painted or traveled since.

And still wouldn't be if it wasn't for Cam. He'd owed Cam and always paid his debts…but this debt was paid in full after this.

"I always did love a man in boots and Wranglers." She squeezed his tense muscle hard and then cooed, "Oh my, that's nice. If my niece wasn't already getting married, I'd get your number for her. Ha—if I was thirty years *young-a,* I'd get it for myself."

Grant stared at the little lady, unsure how to answer her or even whether an answer was appropriate. A dull throb started behind his eyes as he tried to figure out a way to extract his arm from her grasp.

He looked out the window just as the plane touched down. He stared back at the smug-looking lady as the wheels made connection with the runway.

She winked. "And here we are. Safe and sound." She gave his arm one last pat before she calmly folded her hands in her lap. "I hope you're about to enjoy some of this beautiful weather and gorgeous water we have here on the coast."

Still a little delayed reacting, the tension in his body eased as he leaned back into the seat while the plane taxied toward the small airport terminal. "I'm hoping to. I'll be heading over the bridge to Windswept Bay."

"Such a lovely area. It's very quaint in many ways and far less commercialized than St. Pete's. My niece is getting married there next month at the lovely small resort there. Is that where you'll be staying?"

"Yes, ma'am."

"I hear that famous painter of sea life is coming to paint one or two of his beautiful murals on the walls. I can't recall his name, but his work is amazing. It will truly make the quaint resort stand out."

Grant caught himself before he said thank-you— because he was the painter she was referring to. Not keen on revealing his identity to the pint-sized woman who'd just seen him sweat out the plane landing, he kept that information to himself.

Thirty minutes later, after grabbing his gear, he slumped into the backseat of the town car the resort had sent for him and finally relaxed as the car traveled down the highway and at last, over the small bridge to Windswept Bay.

He leaned his head back and stared at the ceiling of the car. He'd made it through the first step.

Now, if he could just make himself paint.

From the cliffs of Lookout Point, Cali Sinclair breathed

in the salty scent of the air as she paused her morning jog to enjoy the beauty from the high vantage point. The blue waters of the bay stretched below her and in the distance, she saw two dolphins jump from the shimmering water in a picture-perfect moment. The beauty of it tugged at her heart.

It was good to be home back on the bay.

She was home and she would never let herself be persuaded to leave again.

When she checked her watch, she realized she'd lingered longer than she'd intended. She headed down the rugged path as she fought off the wave of nerves that she'd hoped the jog would subdue. But nope, the nasty nerves remained like day-old tuna left on the counter—totally and completely impossible to deny any longer. Yes, she was rattled and, despite everything she'd told herself, she knew it was because her first meeting with Grant Ellington was less than an hour away.

Grant Ellington.

Who wouldn't be rattled?

The man's art was incredible. He—the extraordinary, famous artist—was coming here to paint for the resort. She still could not believe that an artist of his caliber was going to fulfill her dream for the resort by creating three murals on their property. And those murals would then be forever part of his impressive portfolio. It was…was…unimaginable.

It was incredible.

She'd been moved by his work for years and though she'd never dreamed it possible to have him do them here, it was his murals that had inspired her to want to add sea life or as some would say, marine life murals to the resort. No, never in a hundred years had she thought the resort would have Grant Ellington originals gracing their walls.

Yes, he was her older brother's neighbor in Texas, but still, it never crossed her mind. For one, they didn't have the money to pay his commission fees. So when Cam had called with the news, she'd been floored. She still was and completely unsure how even Cam had managed something so impossible. And for the price that she and her sisters had put into their budget.

And he would be here soon. Her mind whirled with things she needed to do before meeting him. As she entered the building, she was distracted as she clicked off her list:

Shower and change.

Review her ideas for what she wanted on the two, maybe three sites.

Grab a chocolate bar to hopefully settle her nerves. Probably no time for chocolate, she amended, glancing at her watch while rounding the corner and slamming into an extremely hard male chest. "Humph," she grunted. She staggered back and found herself gaping up into the deep-blue eyes and the sun-bronzed face of Grant Ellington.

McDreamboat as her sister Shar had labeled him because of his Patrick Dempsey dark curls, lean face, and intense eyes. Her breath froze in her throat—he was better-looking than he'd appeared in any of the photos she'd seen of him. And his gaze bored into hers as intense as fire-lit sapphire.

Strong hands tightened on her arms, steadying her physically while completely discombobulating her mentally.

"Sorry, are you all right?" Concern and surprise

rumbled in his deep voice.

"Excuse me. Mr. Ellington, I'm sorry," she said after a moment. "I'm fine. I was in a rush, but I didn't mean to run into you. I was just going up to shower and get ready to meet with you." *Dear goodness, she was rambling.*

He smiled easily. "It's okay, Cali. Everything's fine."

He was gorgeous—she tried not to gape. "How did you know who I was?"

"Pictures." His lips curled upward and he released her, hesitating as if to make sure she wasn't going to fall over.

"Oh," was all she managed. Despite that he'd released her, the feel of his hands on her skin remained as the tingle of awareness from his touch continued to radiate through her and completely disarm her.

"And please call me Grant. Or am I going to be required to call you Ms. Sinclair?"

"Of course not. Grant it is."

"Better. I look around for my dad when someone says Mr. Ellington." He raked a hand through his cropped waves of dark hair and her fingers itched.

Business. Think of business, *not* tingling skin. She cleared her throat. "What picture did you see?"

"Cam has pictures of all of you on his walls at his ranch."

"Oh, right. So, did you get checked in okay?"

"I did, and I was about to go for a walk over the property, get a feel for the surroundings. I'd love for you to come with me."

She glanced down at her jogging attire. "I just came from a run. I really need to change."

"You look great to me. No need to change on my account. What do you say? I'm casual, you're casual."

He wore a T-shirt and cargo shorts and a pair of boat shoes; he looked like one of the vacationers at the resort. A pair of Oakley shades nestled in the dark curls of hair. It was collar length and rich in tone and texture. *Perfect for running one's fingers through*—Cali halted her runaway thoughts with a firm reminder that she was in no way interested in running her fingers through his hair or any man's right now. Or maybe ever.

She'd been through one trial by fire and had no

plans to repeat.

Not even one as enticing as Grant Ellington. So why was she even having this conversation with herself? The man simply wanted her to check out the resort with him.

"What you have on is perfect for showing me around," he continued when she hesitated. "For the murals, I need to see the lay of the land."

"Of course. Sorry." She was hot and sweaty but, she reminded herself, she wasn't trying to impress Grant with anything other than her vision for the resort's murals.

"Great." His gaze flickered over her face as if he were memorizing her every feature.

Absurd. Why would he do that? And why was her pulse rate careening around like lava rocks cascading down a cliffside? On top of that, why was she unable to tear her gaze away from him?

Suddenly, he blinked and his eyes focused, as if coming back from being dazed. He smiled almost hesitantly. "So, where do we start?"

CHAPTER TWO

"I'll show you what you'll be working on." Cali led the way into the main area of the small resort, determined to shake off her fan-girl reaction to Grant.

She focused on the wide-open space that ran from the back entrance to the courtyard, all the way to the front of the resort where registration was located. Several seating areas filled the long, wide space between the entrance and the exit. A long, winding staircase gleaming of dark wood went up to the second floor, where the offices were located. Near the front of the lobby, there was an eighteen-foot-tall wall that she envisioned with an ocean wave, with the varying tones of the gorgeous water gleaming. She could see it in her mind, but her painting skills were limited to the coloring book. She didn't even paint walls.

"This is one of the spaces I'm hoping you'll paint." She looked from the blank wall to him. He placed his hands on lean hips and studied it briefly before he turned to take in the room.

"Nice room. So where to next?"

That was it? "Well, I thought we'd talk about what I want here."

"There's something outside, right?"

"Yes, but on this wall I'd like a bit of beach, but the focus to be a huge wav—"

"I'd prefer to see all of the spaces first before I decide what I want to paint. And I want to get a feel for the whole series before we talk specifics."

"But, I know what I want—"

"Didn't Cam explain that I paint what I'm inspired to paint?"

She hesitated. "Actually, no." This was not the way she'd envisioned it. "My big brother neglected to pass that detail on to us here. Or at least I'm unaware of it if he did."

Cam wasn't a man who forgot anything. So, Cali knew if he had left this detail out, he'd done it on purpose. He knew she had her own ideas for what these walls should have on them.

"That doesn't sound like Cam."

She gave a tight smile. "No, it doesn't." Not unless he neglected to tell her on purpose. *What was her brother up to?*

"Are you all right with this? You just need to trust me."

No, she wasn't all right. Not at all. She'd been off-centered from the moment they'd met and felt as if any moment she was going to roll headfirst down the rocky slope. And trust…oh, trust was a hard one for her, even if it was just about a painting. "I'm fine," she lied, because she couldn't tell him what was really going through her head. She started to bring up her ideas for the wall and then remembered he was doing this for pennies compared to what he normally charged. Her thoughts racing, she said the only safe thing she could think of: "I guess we'll continue the tour."

She led the way toward the beach area. *"You just need to trust me."* Such a common statement with more meaning than most people realized. Especially to someone like her.

She told herself he was not her ex and she had to fight off her instant need to judge him or all men by Paul. The mere thought of her ex disgusted her.

Grant had no idea that trusting any man other than her brothers and her dad was a hard request to make of her. But that was an irrational problem that she was going to have to overcome.

Starting now. If she couldn't trust Grant Ellington, then this project was already doomed.

How would they make it work?

And Cam would be upset with her. He'd explained Grant's situation. She knew he'd been through a horrific tragedy when the plane he'd been flying in had crashed near the runway. There had been three men on the plane and he'd been the only one to live. Cam had told her it had hit Grant hard. She'd been going through her own version of horrible about the same time as she was in the midst of her nasty, long, drawn-out divorce.

Cam had confided that he was worried about his friend. And that this would be his first time to travel from his home since the tragedy. The first time for him to fly, too. Coming here could not have been easy for him.

Determination filled her. They'd make it work. She'd make sure they did.

The plane ride had done a number on Grant. He managed to calm down by the time he'd reached the resort but that didn't mean his head was screwed on straight yet. But, Cam had been right when he'd said Windswept Bay was an inspiring place and could help him ease back into his work. Grant hadn't been interested at first, but then Cam had played the "you *said* you owed me" card.

Ironic, considering Cam didn't really believe Grant owed him anything. It was Grant who insisted that he did and so Cam had known full well that that was the best way to get Grant to make a move.

Grant had made the mistake one evening of telling Cam that he felt dead inside and didn't think he'd ever feel anything again. And that had been when Cam told him that his sisters had taken over running the small boutique resort that had been in their family for several generations. They were making some changes and updates and one of the sisters wanted murals painted on a few strategic areas. That said, Cam had called in Grant's debt.

And that was the only reason Grant was here now.

The verdict was still out on whether he'd be able to paint.

But, as Grant followed the quick-stepping Cali, he was fascinated by her. Mesmerized might be a better word. She was distractingly gorgeous, with her gleaming blonde hair and her sun-kissed skin. She'd been soft in his arms when she'd run headfirst into him; he'd wrapped his arms around her and he'd had a very hard time releasing her.

He was having trouble concentrating. She probably thought he was one odd bird but, after feeling numb for months, when he'd looked down into her eyes, he'd felt alive.

And every time since. He had to force himself not to stare at her. She was like a work of art waiting to happen. Her face was made to be painted.

But she was nervous. Shaken, even. And he'd done that to her.

Had it been because she'd felt the sparks too? Or was it something else?

Cam had told him that one of his four sisters had gone through a really bad divorce. It was hard to keep them all straight because he and Cam mostly talked about ranching. But as Grant rifled through his memory, he was certain it was Cali's name Cam had mentioned with divorce.

As they moved across the courtyard, he couldn't help noticing how pretty it was. Filled with tropical flowers and cobblestone paths, he focused his attention to his surroundings and off Cali. "This is a beautiful place."

"We think so. But, I can only imagine the gorgeous places you've been to and created your work. Our small resort has to be a let-down."

"No, not at all. You don't like your resort?"

"I love it, but it has its shortcomings if compared to world-class resorts. I've seen the places that have commissioned your murals."

"And now you're one of them. I like the smaller, boutique feel of this. Some resorts can be too large and the landscaping too much. These grounds are fantastic."

"I agree. My sister Jillian's responsible for the gorgeous landscape. She'll be pleased that you like her work. I think she's an artist with her plants. I'm a big fan of Jillian's talent. Even if she is my sister and part owner of the resort, we are fortunate to have her as resident landscape artist."

They walked over a small bridge with a man-made lagoon flowing gently beneath it and he could see the pool area ahead of them. There was a very blank wall running across from the pool.

"As you can see, this needs some livening up. The pool is a popular place despite the ocean being just past the courtyard interior. I'd like to bring the ocean here, to those who don't want to actually swim in it."

"It is in need. Is there an outside wall I'm supposed

to paint?"

She nodded and looked back at the blank wall beside the pool. He could tell she wanted to tell him more about her vision of what she wanted on the wall. Instead, she literally bit her bottom lip and held back.

Despite all his efforts, his gaze locked onto her mouth. And suddenly he wasn't thinking about painting.

She was staring at him too. "This way," she said, tersely, as she spun and walked briskly away from him. "It will be visible from the beach and I just think it could be a great statement."

Electricity flowed through his veins. "Your instincts are great." Guilt suddenly tried to swallow him and he tried to focus on anything but how he was affected by her.

Pulling his gaze away from her swaying hips and flouncing ponytail, he forced himself to look at the white sandy beach and the sparkling water. It was a wide beach with waves washing gently onto the sand, where children built sandcastles and adults enjoyed the pristine day.

"This is the largest area and will be seen by so many

people from the beach." Cali swung around.

He ran into her this time.

It happened so suddenly there was nothing he could do. Instinctively, his arms went around her as their feet tangled and to his dismay, they tumbled to the sand.

This was not exactly the way to make a good impression.

But…as he landed in the sand, he knew at this moment he didn't care about anything but that he had Cali in his arms.

Not again! Cali wasn't sure what had happened, just that she turned too quickly and found herself in Grant's arms and fell into the sand, with her landing on top of him.

"Oh," she managed, breathlessly looking down at him. He stared up at her and she could feel his heart pound beneath her hand, where it rested there on his chest. For a moment, they just seemed frozen and then he laughed huskily as he rolled to his side and gently deposited her beside him in the sand. Her heart thundered and it wasn't from the fall or from fear. His arms held her, cocooned in their protective grasp. And then, he smiled…not the partial or hint of a smile she'd seen before but a full-blown, gleaming white smile that knocked her socks off.

Potent. Sexy. Lethal.

"I'd say we need to stop meeting like this, but I'm enjoying it too much." His gaze went back to her lips and her insides melted like honey on a hot day.

She knew she should move. That she needed to escape his arms, but she couldn't.

"Are you okay?" he asked, concern in his tone.

"Fine. I'm just…" *Dear goodness, what was wrong with her?* "I need to get up," she snapped as alarm curled through her. She scrambled away from him, forcing herself out of his arms.

What was wrong with her? She'd sworn off men and now, one moment in Grant's arms and she was all gooey inside. And wanting his kiss?

No. No, ma'am. This wouldn't do.

He sat up, and then rose and pulled her to stand. The brief teasing flirtation that had first flickered through his eyes was gone, replaced with concern. "Are you sure you're all right? The fall didn't hurt you?"

"No. I…I just lost my breath for a moment." It wasn't a lie. She had lost her breath—just not from the fall.

"I'm glad you weren't harmed because of my carelessness."

He gently brushed sand from her cheek, flustering her all the more and making her want to dust him off. "I turned too quickly," she blurted and started dusting herself off like a madwoman batting at attacking bees.

She could feel his perplexed gaze on her but she didn't look at him. Oh no, that would not do because he could probably see her thoughts in her eyes.

"I should have been paying attention." He dusted himself off with easy, normal taps here and there. "I was distracted by the beauty around me."

Her head jerked up. She looked at him and got the enticing notion that he was including her in that beauty. Butterflies the size of parrots went crazy inside her stomach. In defense, she turned back to the building. "This wall will be a feature in the ads for the resort when our new campaign begins," she blurted. "It'll be very important." *This was business. Only business.* She shot him a glance, trying to emphasize the importance his work would make and the fact that she was getting this tour back on track.

But instead of looking at her or the building, he had turned to stare out at the ocean and then the cliffs down the beach. Her gaze, drat it to the moon and back, drank him in like a starving woman.

Anger boiled over inside her as she forced herself to study the view too.

The cliff that rose up on the other end of the resort was striking and she loved to jog and hike up it as part of her workout.

Her gaze wandered back to him; longing flared inside her. She snuffed it out—she'd sworn off men. Sworn off relationships—since she'd been finally freed from her horrible marriage—and now Grant had awakened this dangerous flood of…she refused to call it desire. She'd lost that a long time ago. Hadn't been able to imagine ever wanting another man's hands on her. But…suddenly, all she wanted was to be back in Grant's arms.

His heart raced as Grant studied the landscape and tried not to let his mind linger on what had just happened. Holding Cali for those short few moments had made him want to hold onto her and not let go.

He was here to paint.

To try to feel again—and boy was he. He stared out at the open ocean as conflicting emotions rolled like the waves.

"I don't understand," she snapped.

The anger in her words startled him. He focused on her and saw that her green eyes were alive with it.

"You," she continued with a wave of her hand in his direction. "You barely looked at the wall. *Or* the pool wall. *Or* the main lobby wall. Do you not want this job? You act absolutely bored."

What could he say? How could he tell her that for the first time in months, he felt an emotion other than the hollow sense of emptiness and loss?

That looking at her, holding her, he felt alive.

"This is ridiculous," she muttered before he could

find words. Then she stalked away, her hips swaying with each angry step.

"Wait." He moved quickly to catch up to her and without thinking, he reached for her arm. "Hold on."

Her emerald eyes remained full of fire when she looked back at him.

"Cali, I didn't mean to make you mad. This is just my process."

"I don't understand you."

"I can see that I should have explained better. I work in tandem with the environment around my canvas. To me, a wall is a wall until I paint something on it. Looking at it isn't going to tell me anything. The environment around it will tell me everything. That's what I'm looking for. I know you have ideas for your walls, but you could hire anyone to paint your idea. You can tell me what you want all day long and it won't help me give you what makes my work what it is. Until I experience what you already know and I grow to appreciate it, I won't have a feel for it. And even if I paint it, the wall won't come to life. And that's what you're after. Isn't it?"

Talking about his work explained some of what she'd seen but not all. It at least gave him an excuse for making her uncomfortable.

The anger in her eyes dissipated and the stiffness of her shoulders relaxed. "Why didn't you say that in the first place?"

Looking at her with the beach behind her, he was suddenly thinking of moonlit nights and… He rubbed the back of his neck, biding time as he tried to make sense of what was happening between them. "I get focused on my objective and I sometimes forget that people can't read my mind. Forgive me?" he finished gently.

Seconds ticked by. At last she nodded. "I can understand that. I can do the same thing, or so I'm told by my siblings."

Cam had warned him that he had four sisters and in a half teasing wager, dared Grant not to fall for one of them while he was on this project. Grant had taken his words lightly, but now…now he wasn't so sure Cam hadn't been right. Cali took his breath away. The force of attraction he felt toward her was incredible. And before he'd met her, he'd say that was impossible after the deadness that had been filling him since the crash.

The crash.

The thought sobered him. For a few moments, he hadn't thought about it. Guilt cut through him.

"Let's go up there." He walked, taking long strides, intent on putting some distance between him and the thoughts swirling in his mind. He might be thinking of moonlit nights and kisses but he was here for a job. He had no right to feel anything.

"Grant," she called, startling him. She took a few steps toward him and there was a lost expression in her eyes.

"Is something wrong?"

She shook her head but he didn't believe her.

"I just need to get back, change and get ready for my afternoon agenda. You go ahead and explore and if you need something, I'll be in my office."

She didn't wait for a reply as she headed back toward the resort and left him standing at the base of the path, wondering whether he looked as lost as she had just now.

CHAPTER THREE

Cali's sister Shar looked up from her computer when Cali entered the office.

"Hey, glad you're here. I'm about to head over to the sea turtle hospital and lead a tour. They just brought in an injured big fella that got caught in a fishing li—" She stopped short and her eyes sharpened. "What's wrong? You look…flustered."

"I do not," Cali denied and fought the urge to glance in the mirror near the door. Despite having showered and changed in the hour since she'd abandoned Grant at the beginning of the trail, she still felt shaken by her reaction to the man.

"No." Shar gave a sardonic laugh. "Big sis, you're in a dither. Your cheeks are flushed, you're stomping, and *you*, Miss Cool, never do that. So spill."

A groan rolled through Cali. Shar was not one to let something drop when she thought she was onto something. Still, Cali gave pretending nothing was wrong her best shot. Carefully she pulled her chair up to her desk and turned on her own computer.

She could feel Shar's eyes narrow. Absolutely felt the pinpricks of her stare.

Shar tapped her lip with a finger. "No, something is up. I can feel it through your pretending. Although you should win an Oscar for your performance."

Cali let out an exasperated huff and met her sister's all-too perceptive gaze. "You see too much."

"Thanks. I try. But to be fair, this wasn't too hard to see." Shar laughed and then cut it short and frowned. "It's not about your dirt-bag ex, is it? I tell you, if that sorry excuse for a ma—"

"No, not him. Calm down, Superhero," she urged affectionately. Shar was always rescuing something or someone. If she knew all the details of Cali's life before her divorce, she would have been really upset. But Cali had kept most of her problems to herself, not wanting her large family of three sisters and five brothers, parents, and close-knit extended family to know the dirty details. She told herself it was to protect them and keep them from trying to harm Paul, but it was also because she was ashamed. All of this was reminders of exactly why her response to Grant was so unreasonable. At last she snapped, "It's Grant Ellington. The man is…"

Shar's face brightened. "*McDreamboat*—I knew it. You've already seen him!"

"Stop calling him that."

"He is and I will not. All those *make-me-wanna-run-my-fingers-through-it* dark curls and that crooked Patrick Dempsey smile makes a girl's heart go pitter-patter just thinking about it. You can't stop a runaway freight train when the brakes go out."

Cali frowned, because it was all true. Even the pitter-patter part. She just hadn't expected it to be full-blown explosive in person.

"What's he like? I know he checked in late last night." Her eyes widened. "You *have* met him." She stood up in her excitement. "And that's why you're all flustered and—"

"Aggravated. I am not flustered."

Her sister started to say something but her mouth dropped open and she clapped her hands together. "You're *interested*. Praise God! You are actually interested. That's life in them thar eyes that I see."

Cali glared at her. "I'm not—"

"You are too. It's okay if you are, Cali."

Her insides balled up in a knot, causing a dull ache. She knew it was okay to think about another man and to have a new relationship if she chose. She didn't choose. It wasn't that easy. Shar just didn't understand. "I know that, Shar." She wished she could just go crawl under a rock.

"So what happened? Tell me all about it." Shar perched on the edge of Cali's desk. She looked momentarily like the kid sister who'd always waited up for Cali to come home from a date. Back then, she would rush into Cali's room and jump onto her bed and demand to hear all the details of the date. Back then, Cali had liked having someone to talk to about her hopes and dreams and girlish romantic notions. A girl could dream all she wanted to about romance and how perfect her life and love would turn out…but she'd learned the hard way that wolves could hide behind the shiny armor that a knight in shining armor wore while dating. The ugly came out after the vows were said.

These days, she just didn't feel like talking about her sordid past and misplaced trust. The reminder had Cali glaring at her sister—who, as far as Cali knew, had never had a serious relationship in her life. Cali wasn't sure why that was, considering she was always interested in everyone else's love life.

"Come on, give me the details," Shar pressed.

"This is the problem with having so many siblings. The brothers are protective and the sisters are nosey. Especially you." Cali had been away long enough that she'd forgotten just how nosey they could be. There could be more inquisitions if she let on that she was interested.

But she wasn't. She wouldn't let herself be.

Shar made a face. "Yes, I missed my calling as a writer for the *National Enquirer*. Now stop stalling. Did he like your ideas? Did he like you?" She waggled her eyebrows on the last part. "It appears you liked him."

Cali pushed Shar's leg. "Stop it. He didn't want to hear my ideas. He barely looked at the walls where he'll be painting the murals. Said he needs to get the feel for the place."

"That makes sense. Now, about those McDreamboat lips up close and personal. Did you want him to kiss you senseless and have his way with you?"

"*Nooo.*" Cali glared at Shar. "Who are you? The things that you say sometimes boggle my mind." It was the truth: Shar was offbeat and loved to tease. But now was not the time. And she certainly didn't want to be reminded that she'd had thoughts of kissing when she'd been near Grant…in his arms, rolling in the sand.

"You're blushing." Shar gasped and peered at her. "*Seriously* blushing. He *did* want to have his way with you."

"He did *not!* Now stop. Don't you have a tour to lead? A turtle to rescue?"

"Not for another hour. I'm yours for another thirty minutes at least."

"Gee, I'm *so* lucky," Cali muttered just as Jillian walked in.

"What's up?" She walked into the room, carrying a vase of fresh cut Hibiscus.

"Pink Hibiscus." Shar looked from the flowers to Cali and grinned. "Oh look, Cali, just your color."

Jillian peered at her. "Why are you the same color as my Hibiscus blooms?" she exclaimed and of course Shar nearly collapsed with laughter.

"Okay, what's up?" Jillian looked from laughing Shar to frowning Cali.

"I think Cali likes our Mr. McDreamboat."

"Ellington," Cali snapped. "How old are you anyway?"

Shar sobered. "Old enough to know what I'm seeing. The question is why are you denying that you saw a great guy, are obviously attracted to the man, and are denying it with all your heart?"

"Yes, why?" Jillian placed her hands on her jean-clad hips, fully alerted now. "Your divorce was final months ago—thank the good Lord. You're allowed to find men attractive, especially after what you went through. And don't try to deny it. I know there's more to the story than you are letting on. I'm thrilled to see those blushing cheeks and a bit confused as to why you're so hesitant." She gave Shar a pointed look. "Stop teasing her. We don't understand it but this is obviously hard for Cali."

Cali stood and had to fight the desire to run. Literally. Running soothed her tattered nerves and helped her go numb while she was tracking steps. Running helped her cope.

"I'm fine." She was. Really. "You're both right. I've been flustered from the moment I met him this morning. And despite what you think, I don't want to be. I need to get my life back on track. To be cool with myself for a long while before I even think about opening up to another man. Or if I ever will. It's a risk I really don't want to take."

"I get that to a point," Jillian said. "I have my own walls that I'm not ready to climb over but I guess I was hoping for you the process might be sped up. All you've done since coming home is bury yourself in work. You move through the days but there isn't any light in you."

"Right now there is," Shar interjected.

"I enjoy the work and there's a lot to do."

"True," Shar said, "but it is a tropical paradise, so you need to stop and dig your toes into the sand some. And for crying out loud, when something or someone piques your interest, pursue it."

"She's right, Cali." Jillian headed for the coffee. "So tell us what happened."

Cali gave up. "I ran into him downstairs." She omitted that she meant literally slammed into him. "He wanted to see the walls but then he just didn't seem to pay attention to them. He wants to get the feel for the place. He won't even listen to my ideas at this point." She let out a frustrated breath as her sisters watched her as if she were on the movie screen. All they needed was popcorn. "It's frustrating." She did not tell them about rolling in the sand...the very remembrance had her insides going fluttery.

Her sisters were both smiling when she finished.

"You left him at the base of Lookout Point?" Jillian

asked.

"Yes. I had things to do."

"Why do I get the feeling you left something out?" Shar asked with an all-too knowing expression.

Jillian tugged at her ear. "This is going to be an interesting few weeks, I think."

Goose bumps prickled Cali's skin at the idea. "There is nothing going on, you two. Grant Ellington is here to paint, not be my boyfriend."

There was a knock on the wooden frame of the open door. Everyone turned to find Grant standing there, in all of his amazing glory.

Cali's pulse fluttered and she tried for a poker face to conceal her reaction from her nosey sisters.

"Well, hello, *Gorgeous*," Shar drawled and stood. "Come on in. We're excited you're here." She winked at Cali and then grinned back at Grant.

Cali groaned and tried not to look guilty of talking about the man. It hit her then: what if he'd heard them as he approached the doorway? She quickly reviewed what had been said in the moments before he knocked on the door and remembered her adolescent boyfriend declaration.

This was a disaster that just kept growing.

CHAPTER FOUR

As he stood in the doorway of the offices of the Windswept Bay Resort, Grant caught the flicker of worry that crossed Cali's face the moment she realized he was there. He'd heard her boyfriend remark just before knocking on the door. He had a feeling she'd realized he'd probably heard that remark. She hid the worry—or was that guilt?—he saw in her eyes before she shot him a weak smile. Something was up. Her words had to have been due to something her sisters had said; otherwise, he couldn't imagine her just coming out and saying something like that. And yet the idea of being her boyfriend or more had him instantly thinking about moonlit beaches and holding hands and kisses.

He needed to get those thoughts out of his head. But, right now, looking at how lovely she looked, it wasn't happening.

Instead of saying something to Cali first, he decided it might be best to speak to her sisters first. He turned his focus on the beautiful woman with the short, curly brown hair and the teasing eyes who'd called him gorgeous.

He chuckled as he commented on her observation, "I don't know about the gorgeous statement but I'm excited to be here." He moved into the room and placed the picnic hamper he was carrying on the desk. It was past lunch but that didn't matter at the moment. "You must be Shar. And I believe you must be Jillian," he said to the beautiful blonde, whose long hair was tied loosely at the nape of her neck with a colorful scarf.

The brunette laughed. "Gorgeous and you've done your homework."

"You've guessed correctly," Jillian said, her eyes warm. "But then, since you're a friend of Cam's, I'm thinking maybe you've seen our pictures…" She hitched a quizzical eyebrow.

He smiled. "Cam's not a huge talker but he has mentioned all of you and I have seen pictures. Even if not, Cali mentioned your talents with the landscape, Jillian, and you've got a little dirt on your knees."

She laughed, a delightful sound, soft and earthy like her as she glanced down at her knees. "You got me. I was digging in the dirt a few minutes ago. I can't seem to help myself."

"Gorgeous and observant," Shar said with a sassy grin before he could reply to Jillian. "So what's in the picnic basket? I'm the nosey one, if you haven't yet figured it out."

Till now, Cali had remained quiet as she watched him with her sisters. He looked at her and hoped she was up for his suggestion. "I'm here to paint murals for the resort and like I told Cali, I like to be inspired by the area before I know what to paint. I thought it would be good to tour the island. And a guide would be nice." He directed the comment to Cali. Her eyes narrowed instantly. Wariness or curiosity? He wasn't sure what it was but she was listening. "I thought you would be the perfect guide since you're the one who has a strong idea of what you believe should be on those blank walls."

"That's a great idea!" Shar exclaimed. "Cali, you do know your vision. Now you can convince Grant that it's the right vision. You can inspire him."

"It's perfect." Jillian agreed.

Grant watched her sisters gang up on Cali. By the look of horror on her face, he wasn't sure whether to be insulted by her reaction or concerned for her.

She would kill her sisters later.

Completely aghast that they looked so overjoyed at the idea, Cali fought for calm and unruffled. "But, I can't. I have work—"

"You have work, yes you do," Shar snapped, sending a determined look Cali's way. "Helping design the walls that will draw people to the resort. You have very important work. This resort needs something eye-catching to set it apart and Grant is absolutely right—he needs someone to help him find that inspiration. You're the one for the job and since I'm sure he doesn't have a lifetime to spend on our project alone, you need to get on it right now."

"Shar and I can handle anything that comes up." Jillian walked around the end of the desk to stand beside Cali. When Cali made no move, she nudged her in the ribs. "*Go.* We're very lucky to have Grant doing this for us. The least we can do is show him the island."

Grant could tell that Cali was feeling a little hemmed-in by her sisters' enthusiasm. He had his own reservations about spending time alone with her.

He hadn't felt anything in so long and he didn't feel he had a right to feel anything like he felt just looking at her, much less when he touched her. But right now, he couldn't help himself. If he was going to be able to paint, he needed all the help and inspiration he could get.

"I'll go," she said at last, and then, sounding very prim and businesslike, she added, "We are grateful that you agreed to come and do this. So, I'll do whatever you need to get the job done. But, I'm still not comfortable paying you so little compared to the far greater price I'm sure you normally ask."

He'd told Cam he'd do it for the cost of room and board on the island but Cam had insisted that the resort wanted to pay the sum they'd budgeted for the project. He'd agreed to that but planned to find a charity or something to hand over the money to.

"Like I said in my email, I owe Cam. I would have done it for room and board only, but he insisted on payment."

"And he should have. He denies that you owe him anything. That said, you two seem to both be stubborn, so it's worked out for the resort either way."

"It's the Texan in us." He grinned, because it was true.

Shar cocked her head. "You're probably right. He might not have been born in Texas but as he says, he got there as fast as he could." She laughed. "Are you the same way?"

"I was born in Texas and love it there, but I also have sea legs. I love the water."

Jillian smiled. "Cam always says a cowboy can have interests outside the ranch. No wonder you two are friends. I have a feeling you're good on a horse, though. You'll have to get Cali to show you her riding. She's good."

That took him by surprise. "You ride?"

That becoming rose tinged Cali's high cheekbones. "No. Not anymore." She glared at her sisters. Jillian and Shar just smiled.

Grant felt for the poor soul who fell in love with Shar. She'd keep the poor guy on his toes. He liked her vibrant personality and he liked Jillian too, but something about Cali took his breath away every time he looked at her.

"So go. Take him to the falls," Jillian urged. "You know you always loved that place."

"And have a good time," Shar demanded.

Cali sighed. "Fine. We'll go to the falls." She picked up her purse and slung it over her shoulder in a not-so-gentle manner as she walked past him. At the door, she paused to look over her shoulder. "Coming?"

The smile that unfurled inside him was huge. He

picked up the basket. "Ladies," he said and followed her out the door.

His creative mind churned as he followed her down the winding staircase. Her slender fingertips trailed along the dark, gleaming banister. She didn't pause as she stormed down a side corridor, through a door and into the sunlight.

They were in a parking lot on the side of the resort. The brilliant sunshine had him pulling his shades from his head and placing them on his eyes. The scent of Jillian's tropical flower gardens filled the air. But he was focused on the long, fluid movements of Cali as she headed toward a white, roofless Jeep. She tugged off the casual jacket she'd worn with her sundress and tossed it in the back before she pulled out a pair of shades from her purse and then dropped it beside the jacket. She jammed the shades over her green eyes and then climbed into the driver's seat. Clearly she was miffed, as his mom would say. There was fire beneath that calm exterior and he liked it.

He set the basket in the backseat, taking his time before he hopped into the passenger seat beside her.

"Nice ride. Is it yours?"

"It is. You seem surprised."

"I am." He chuckled, something he'd been doing a lot since meeting her. "I'll admit I didn't picture you in an off-road ride."

"I didn't picture you in cargo pants."

He laughed again and couldn't help himself. "And how exactly did you picture me?"

To his surprise, she laughed finally. "In jeans and boots, wearing a Stetson, like you are on your website. Which, I will admit, seemed at odds with the sea life that you're famous for."

"Sorry to disappoint you. These cargoes work better for island life. And as Jillian pointed out, cowboys do not always fit the stereotype."

"Point taken." She looked at him across her shoulder; even through the pale amber shades, her eyes sparkled in the sunlight with a hint of mischief. "Buckle up, Cowboy. You wanted me to show you the island. So now, we're going for a ride."

He did as he was told. This had the makings of a great day.

The man aggravated her—and also drove her to want to let her hair down.

That was something she hadn't done in such a long time.

Cali had been uptight and somewhat withdrawn from parts of herself ever since the divorce. A divorce, she'd learned, despite her usually strong self-confidence, had a way of stripping everything away and leaving a person feeling bared and lacking. Even her.

She'd once been more adventurous—thus her Jeep—but now it was only when she was alone that she felt the zing of herself wanting to bust out of the cage. But then she'd question her bad choices and know that adventurous side of herself had helped get her into the mess she'd made of her life.

So many wrong choices. Funny how life had a way of whittling a person down.

Today, something felt different. She actually squealed the tires as she cut the corner out of the parking lot and headed for the tallest spot on the small island. It was one of Windswept Bay's hidden gems.

The rush of the salty air and the heat of the sun calmed her.

"You like this?" Grant called over the wind that swirled around them as she drove down the street.

A stop sign had her pressing the brake. When she came to a halt behind another car, she looked at him. "I do. But I'm in the office most of the time."

"This suits you. Do you rock climb?"

"No. I used to hike. I've never gotten a thrill from hanging off the side of a mountain by a thin rope and a hook that I nailed into a crack in the rock." She laughed and shifted gears as she moved through the intersection. A few people on the sidewalks waved as they passed and she waved back. "How about you? You're a beach-painting cowboy from Texas. What else contradictory do you do? Climbing mountains would go against stereotype."

He laughed. "Nope. I'm the same way. I get out of the saddle long enough to paint, but other than flying in a plane…" He paused briefly and she glanced at him, saw his jaw tighten. "Other than flying, my feet are planted firmly to the ground. Hiking is great, though. We're on the same page."

The crash. It was obvious the mention of flying had caused his hesitation. She found herself wanting to ask him about the crash, about how he was doing but she held back. She wasn't ready to get so personal. "My sister Olivia, she's horribly afraid of heights. It's a phobia and drives her crazy. Thankfully, I'm not like that. I just like control too much to trust—" She broke off, realizing, despite not planning to or wanting to, that she was revealing more about herself than she was comfortable with.

She looked straight ahead, feeling Grant's gaze on her as she headed through the tiny town with its touristy sidewalk wares, colorful buildings filled with fudge shops, ice cream, and coffee shops. *Why had she talked so much?* The man was here to paint and then he would leave. She was simply the woman who was overseeing his time here.

"The town's nice."

She glanced at him, relieved that he wasn't asking her more questions about herself considering she'd left the door wide open for them. "Yes, it's your typical tourist town. At least Main Street is. The regular business places and shops are farther down the street or on the side streets."

"So how busy does the island get?"

"Not as busy as it could. That's one reason we are renovating the resort. We can bring in more tourists if we can offer a more up-to-date boutique setting that caters to a wider demographic. Some Grant Ellington artistry will go a long way on moving us up on the destination meter."

They were out of the town now and headed along the coast. "This road winds around the entire island— all twenty miles of it. Though most people drive back the way they went. There is an area along the southern tip of the island that is passable but only for the adventure seekers. It's fairly treacherous in areas. Believe it or not, we get some tourists here just for that stretch of land. We're wanting to reach as wide a group as possible. To have something for everyone—and that begins with special accommodations and experience at the resort."

"Cam told me the town struggled some. I'm not sure my murals are going to be the saving grace, though. That's a lot of pressure."

She glanced at him. "In the words of Shar—gorgeous *and* humble. Hang on." She cut off the main road and hit a dirt road that immediately began a climb up the dirt trail. "You know you and your name have clout." She held the steering wheel with both hands as the road was rough.

Grant had straightened in his seat and was clearly enjoying the ride. She could practically see his interest.

"What I know is I paint pictures that engage people and seem to touch people. Whether it increases revenue, I can't guarantee."

She took her foot off the accelerator. "You're serious, aren't you?"

His forehead creased as concern filled his eyes. "Yeah, I am. So far, what I've seen of the island has been beautiful. And it's an ideal place for a vacation away from the hustle and bustle. But don't bank your renovation on me. On my work."

She now pressed the brake and stared at him. "Well,

I'm not placing all my hopes and dreams for the place on you, but I am placing some of it. I didn't just hire any ole painter." She was serious, but half teasing him when she realized he looked truly troubled.

She turned off the Jeep and unbuckled her seat belt. "Hey, relax. Don't look so troubled. You said you wanted to be inspired and if that's what you need to be totally on board, then follow me." *What was wrong with him? Cam had said he hadn't painted since the crash. Was that part of why he'd seemed so agitated just now?*

Instead of getting out, he removed his shades and, squinting in the sun, he stared at her. "I'm serious, Cali. You and your sisters have obviously put a lot of thought into this renovation to the resort and your 'why' for doing it is a great one. Don't get me wrong. I'm on board but—don't bet the bank on me."

"You're really blowing me away. Are you really not confident?"

"I'm confident that I'll give you something your guests will find pleasure looking at. But hoping it will be the thing that sets you apart and makes you a destination is just not what I do. You need to make sure you have more. And the truth is you do. I'm guessing the waterfall is through those trees?"

"You are so correct. This way. And don't worry, we haven't put all our bets on you."

"Good. Is there a place to set up our late lunch where you're taking me?" He reached into the back of the Jeep and lifted the small hamper. "Or is it better that we see it and then eat when we get back to the Jeep?"

He looked like an ad for every girl's dream date, standing there looking at her with those intense eyes and a quizzical smile on his lips.

Oh wow.

She was in tune with the forest and very aware of the sounds of birds echoing through the trees and the muted sound of the falls that only someone who knew what they were listening for could hear. But above everything, she was aware of the canopy of leaves overhead locking her into very private surroundings with Grant.

The gorgeous, intriguing man was what she was most aware of. He smiled and her heart thundered.

"You can bring it. I'm sure there's room

somewhere." She didn't stop to analyze her thoughts; instead, she headed into the woods, following the well-worn path that led through the tropical landscape and then headed down a steep path. She could feel Grant behind her and wondered whether he could tell that he got to her. The musty scent of damp ground and clean, sweet air filled her lungs. And the ever-so enticing scent of his aftershave.

She'd known him for less than five hours and every moment in his presence was making it harder and harder to focus on anything but him. It was disturbing, to say the least.

He was handsome in a way that appealed to her more than she could understand. She'd seen plenty of gorgeous men in her life and many since her divorce, but she'd never been so instantly drawn to a man.

Since her divorce, she'd not felt anything toward any man.

No, instead, she'd been determined to keep her distance from all men. And now, as she tromped down the path through the plants, she felt a sense of anticipation about having lunch with him in the most romantic spot on the island.

Not that she was going to let him know that.

CHAPTER FIVE

The soft, lush roar of the falls grew the closer they got. Because this was a small fall and not Niagara Falls, it was a sound that set the tone for romance.

Okay, Cali, stop with the romance, would you please?

"We're almost there," she called over her shoulder, more to take her mind off her thoughts than to warn him.

"Sounds good. But I'm enjoying the hike."

The man was in great shape and there was no way this short hike was making him hope the journey would end soon. She led the way around a curve, pushed a banana leaf out of her way and held it back as he moved to stand beside her. His arm touched hers as he moved up beside her. Energy bolted through her like a power surge and the goose bumps she'd had earlier came back in full force. The waterfall was a gentle roar.

"Beautiful," he said, leaning close to her ear.

Grant's warm breath sent a shiver of awareness through Cali and she shifted instinctively toward him. The action brought his body closer to hers as her pulse crashed fast and furiously off the charts. Her mouth went dry and she could only nod as words stuck in her throat.

"Is this place special to you?"

Unable to stop herself, she turned her head toward him and found herself very closely face to face with him. The call of a tropical bird echoed from the trees, emphasizing the sense of them being completely alone in paradise. She couldn't move. Not an inch. Not a finger. Not an eyelash. He made no move either, just held her gaze as time stalled.

"You're beautiful," he whispered at last.

A shiver raced over her and, thankfully, she forced

her feet to move and she stepped away, driven by the need for space.

What was wrong with her? She had just met Grant and yet she had to fight the urge to throw herself into his arms. It was not like her to feel such reckless emotions. Especially after all she'd been through.

And yet she wanted to fall into his arms and—

She wrapped her arms around herself and forced the thoughts out of her mind. She should have never brought him to this spot. She should have never told him to bring the picnic lunch.

"Are you all right?" That concern etched his expression again and he reached to touch her arm.

"I'm fine. Just…" What could she say? "Just hungrier than I thought I'd be. What do you have inside that basket?" It was the only thing she could come up with.

"Hopefully something you'll enjoy. Where should we sit?"

"There's an alcove at a midway point of the falls. There is plenty of room there."

"Then lead on. You've got my attention." In the

shade of the forest, they'd both removed their shades and now, his beautiful blue eyes sparkled with a surprisingly playful glint.

And suddenly, Cali felt reckless.

The gentle fall of the water over the cliff, near where they'd decided to stop to eat, sounded peaceful as Grant reached into the basket and pulled out a couple of bottles of water. He, on the other hand, was as far from peaceful as he could get as he handed a cold bottle to Cali. Their fingers touched and the jolt of electricity that seemed to go with being near her zinged through him.

Unnerved by the continuing reaction to her, he concentrated on pulling a bowl of fresh fruit from the basket. He handed it to her and then pulled out one for himself. Then he pulled out a plate of assorted cheeses and crackers and thinly sliced deli meats.

"You thought of everything," she said.

"I try," he answered, liking the surprise he heard in her voice. "I wasn't sure if you were a vegetarian or maybe gluten-free so I went with caution."

A soft smile lifted the corners of her mouth. "You are a very thoughtful man. I'm neither but it was a nice thought."

He liked that smile. "There's more in here, if you want something else. I didn't want to overwhelm you. Then again, compared to other picnics you might have been on, I didn't want to come up on the short end of the stick either."

"I've never done something like this before."

He paused pulling out a container. "You've never been on a picnic?"

"Not—" She halted, and turned crimson. The woman could blush like nothing he'd ever seen. "I mean, with my family, certainly."

"Oh, you meant with a date."

She fidgeted. "This isn't a...a date."

She was cute. "No, I guess not. But I'm still in shock that no man took you on a picnic. Are the men in Windswept Bay blind? Or just stupid?"

"Well, ah…" Her brows bunched together and then she let out a soft laugh. "I don't have a clue. You really throw me off."

"You look really pretty in pink."

Her fingers went to her cheek. "It's a curse I've suffered with all my life."

"Aw, and I thought it was just me who brought it out in you." He wasn't sure what had come over him. It had been months since he'd felt like himself, but since being around her, his old self kept jumping out with these bad one-liners.

"So are you being inspired?"

He couldn't look away from her. "That's a loaded question but yes, I am. Very much so. Cam didn't tell me I was going to be mesmerized by one of his sisters. Well, he did dare me not to fall in love with one of you but I thought he was joking."

She stiffened and the color drained from her face. "I… Look, Grant. I need to be up-front with you. I appreciate that you're a nice guy, personable, and you believe in repaying a debt you believe you owe my brother. I'm grateful for the opportunity to work with you but I need to be blunt—I'm not on the market. I've been through a divorce several months ago and believe me, I'm not interested in a repeat. I came strictly to show you the island so you can be inspired. Just like you requested."

He put a fork into the melon in his bowl and berated himself for being so insensitive. "I apologize for pushing. I wasn't thinking. I take it your divorce was a rough one?"

She didn't say anything for a moment and he wanted to kick himself for his thoughtlessness.

"It's none of your business, but yes. It was rough." She pulled a grape from the bowl and placed it in her mouth. She chewed slowly while she studied the waterfall, lost in thought.

"Have you ever been married?" she asked at last.

"No. I'm thirty-two and have never even been tempted to marry. I'm not sure if that says something bad about me."

"I think being able to wait until you find the right person is great. But in reality, who actually knows, until the deed is done, if it's going to work out."

"That's pretty cynical." He shouldn't have been surprised after what she'd obviously been through.

"Absolutely. And I really hate it, but that's all I can

feel right now and it goes against my normal nature. Being lost inside yourself is a bad thing," she finished softly.

He knew this was something she didn't share with many people. He could tell by the way she said it. He reached across and laid his hand over hers. "You just need time."

She released a ragged breath and didn't make a move to pull away. "Maybe. If I focus on the resort, it helps me step outside my problems and it's better. I came home because I needed to have some new direction to my life. This resort means the world to me in so many ways."

He could look at her all day. Get lost in the emotions of her eyes and the silken sound of her voice. But mostly he could get lost in helping her find her way back to the woman he knew she so desperately was searching for. Her confession helped him see that but then he felt it too. Maybe it was because he could relate. He hadn't been the same since the crash and didn't think he ever would be. A part of him wanted to be the man he'd once been—but then, a part of him couldn't cross that line. Couldn't let go of what had happened. Of what had been lost.

But this wasn't about him. He gave her hand a gentle squeeze; he'd give her what he could give. "Not the same thing, but I don't know if you know that I recently lived through a plane crash?"

"I did know that. And I wanted to tell you that I was sorry for the loss of your friends. I just didn't want to bring it up because I know it has to be hard for you. What a horrible tragedy it was. And awful to live through."

"Thank you. They were good men who didn't deserve to die. Their loss and the crash…changed me. I can't imagine that I'll ever get back to the person I was before, but, like you, I'm trying to find my footing in the new reality. It's not easy. Coming here is my first step toward moving on." Reluctantly, he released his hold on her. "You're going to come out of this stronger and even more dynamic than the woman I've already come to know. You inspire me."

"Thank you, but…" She halted, as if to pull herself back. A curtain seemed to fall over her gaze. "I brought you here so you'd be inspired by the falls."

He forced himself not to cup her cheek because it was so obvious that she was fighting to stay distant. "Believe me, I've been inspired more than you realize."

"Fine, but I need a painting and the last thing I want is a painting of me."

He laughed hard at the sternness of her tone. "Relax, you'll get your paintings."

The laughter felt good.

Cali plopped another grape into her mouth and chewed; it was the best way she could hide the smile that she wanted to allow herself. It was a defensive move. Grant had gotten to her and she couldn't let him know how much. He seemed to understand her in ways that she was not going to analyze right now. "So, tell me about why you said you owe Cam. He never said anything about you owing him. Only that he mentioned the renovation project to you and my vision for having murals and you offered to do them. I will say that I was surprised when he called and gave me your number. And told me you were flying out here so quickly."

He placed a piece of cheese on a cracker and then doubled a slice of turkey and handed it to her. She thanked him and then watched as he made his.

"Cam wouldn't tell you because he keeps telling me that he did what anyone would have done. He saw a grass fire heading toward my house and he put himself in danger to protect my home. He was hurt in the process. My stuff isn't worth someone getting harmed over. I was grateful the house and my belongings were saved, but he's worth more than stuff. I owed him."

"I see. Of course he neglected to tell me that. He didn't come out here while he had the injury. None of us knew he'd even been hurt. Mom and Dad went to visit him and saw the scar on his arm and that was the first we knew of it."

"Sounds like him. He denies vehemently that he did anything heroic, and I kid him and tell him he's right— it was idiotic. His life is worth more. Still I owe him."

"And the resort is benefiting."

"I think it's a perfect solution. This meant a lot to him, helping all of you get the resort going, and his plan was to pay me the difference of what you had budgeted. I flat-out refused doing the job if that was the case, so we finally compromised and I'm accepting the payment."

"But then donating it."

"It's a win-win. Don't you think?"

She had to admit that it was.

CHAPTER SIX

"So tell me about yesterday," Shar demanded the moment she saw Cali the next day.

"It was great. He's a nice man." A man she hadn't stopped thinking about all night.

Shar's mouth dropped open. "A nice man. That's all I get? Are you kidding me? I want details. Did you kiss him?"

"Oh, for Pete's sake," Cali snapped. "Are *you* kidding me? I'm not going to kiss the man. Why are you even asking that?"

"Because I *want* you to. You need your life shaken

up some. Grant Ellington seems to be the man who might be able to do exactly that. Just because you got a bad apple on the first go-round doesn't mean it's time to give up on all men."

No way was she letting on that she hadn't been able to stop thinking about Grant.

"You're thinking about him right now! You're turning pink and Grant's the man who causes that reaction in you."

"What—" Cali glared in denial at Shar just as Jillian walked by the door. "Jillian, come in here," she demanded.

"Boy, do you look flustered," Jillian said. "Get that from your afternoon with a certain handsome man?"

That did it. "Okay, look you two, we need some boundaries. I'm just going to say this once. You two need to stop pushing."

Jillian cleared her throat. "I haven't been pushy. I just hope you'll not shut yourself off from doing something for yourself, like exploring possibilities with someone you're attracted to."

Cali knew there was no hiding it from her sisters.

"Fine. I am attracted to him." She moved to the door and closed it, not taking any chances on Grant walking up and overhearing her conversation. It would be too embarrassing and it just simply wasn't good. He might get the wrong impression. She turned back to her sisters and shot a very pointed look at Shar.

"I don't know what to do. There, are you both satisfied? I went through a horrible divorce, a betrayal that rocked me to my core. I'm scared but I can't stop thinking about him."

Shar gave her a hug. "It's okay to be scared. It means you're taking a risk, pushing past boundaries that are trying to hold you back. It's a good thing."

"I don't know," Cali murmured.

"Cali." Jillian's voice was gentle. "You can do this. You are in control. If you realize you aren't comfortable or this isn't what you want, then pull back. But at least you'll have stretched yourself and moved past a barrier."

"And that's all I want for you." Shar rubbed her arm. "That you're happy. I want my sister back."

"I get that. I am happy, but you might have to settle

for this me. Both of you are single and seem to be happy about it. Olivia is single and loving her life. And then we haven't even gotten to our brothers. All four of them are as busy as can be and seem to be fine. I'm the only one who married and failed and now I'm happy, thrilled even, to be single again. I don't understand why the two of you seem to think I need a man to make me happy."

Jillian looked thoughtful. "I think all of us—well, maybe not some of the brothers—but most of us are willing to admit that we're getting of the age that we would welcome the right person coming along. I'm all for it. I really would love to start a family. And Shar, she's—"

Shar cut her off with a laughing declaration. "Is not ready."

Cali's mouth dropped open. "Then why are you pushing me?"

"Because the man makes you pink. I've been saying that all along. You are never pink. You are a calm, cool, collected gal with your act together who used to like to have fun. Your jerky ex-husband rattled your existence and stole something from you that you need to get back. Your mojo…your confidence—the thing that made you sparkle. You are a smart, sexy, desirable woman, who's a fun and genuinely good person. Who got pushed off the path. Pink tells me things. Tells me that this guy is shaking up your world in a good way. It's time to get your mojo back."

Cali could not help chuckling. If there was one thing about her sister Shar, it was that she was brash and always would be a cheerleader. "Okay, I get it, Dr. Lovejoy. You should get your own late-night radio show. You could put the real Dr. Lovejoy out of business."

"Yeah, right. I'll stick with giving you advice and let the mysterious Dr. Lovejoy have everyone else."

"That's probably a good thing," Jillian told her and then looked at Cali. "Yesterday was a good start for you. Now, keep it up. Go for it."

"Perfectly said, sister," Shar drawled.

"So is he taking you anywhere today?" Jillian asked.

She shot her sisters a face of mild exasperation. "Hopefully, he starts painting today. Remember, that's what he's here for." She was tired of the focus on her personal life.

"That's true." Jillian's expression said she got the hint. "I just came from the beach area and the scaffold has been set up for the beach wall. The crate of supplies is in the gardening supply area but it's unopened."

He'd asked Cali whether she would be available today and she'd told him she would be. However, so far she found herself wondering what he was doing. Or where he was.

"Maybe you should go check on him. This is, after all, your project to handle."

"You're right," Cali agreed with mixed emotions. It was her project. She headed toward the door. Her sister looked so innocent but Shar had found the push button needed to get her to make a move when she'd reminded Cali that this was business. "If he comes by here, let him know I'm looking for him."

"Oh, we will," they said in unison.

Cali didn't bother to answer them but instead gave a wave over her shoulder as she headed into the hallway and down the stairs.

Horace Finley, the maintenance man, looked down from the ladder where he was repairing a light fixture. "Smile, Cali girl. You look like you just smelled bad fish."

She laughed. "Gee, thanks, Horace."

"Oh, no thanks needed. Just telling it like I see it. But, see'n how you've got that look on your face already, maybe I might as well break the bad news to you. The AC unit is on its last leg. Sorry to be the bearer of bad news."

Cali's shoulders slumped. "Are you sure?"

"I've patched it again, but it ain't holding refrigerant and the motor's ancient. It's probably not going to make it through the busy season."

Just what she needed. When she'd agreed to go in with her sisters and take over running the resort, her dad had warned them that there were some major expenses coming because of the age of the place. This was one of them. It would be thousands of dollars to put in a new central unit on the main building. And then there were the rooms with their aging units. "You did warn me,

Horace," she said, weakly. "Um, thanks. I guess."

He shrugged. "If it ain't one thing, it's another."

"Thanks, Horace. That's a true comfort."

"Just doin' my job, little lady. I'll keep her running as long as I can—you just need to know the end is coming. Sorry."

"I know. It's not your fault. You do a miraculous job and we appreciate it. Dad has always called you Superman. And he's right."

He bowed out his chest. "Not quite filling out my uniform like I used to back in the day."

Despite the news he'd just handed her, she smiled up at him. "You might be seventy but you look every bit of fifty."

He huffed. "Now you've gone to flat-out lying and I know for a fact that your mom taught you better."

She laughed. "True. I'll see you later. And I'll start looking into air conditioners." Trying not to think of the dollars she was going to have to find somewhere, somehow, she headed outside to the pool area but Grant wasn't there. Then she headed out to the exterior wall.

As Jillian had told her, the scaffolding was erected but Grant wasn't on it. She stared at the water for a moment and fought off the burden of the monstrous central unit she was about to have to buy. It felt as though it was sitting squarely on her shoulders. Shaking it off, she strode back to the lobby and stopped at the house phone to dial Grant's room.

He picked up on the first ring. "Oh, you're there," she said.

He chuckled. "I'm here. Am I not supposed to be?"

"Sorry." She rubbed her temple. "I didn't mean to snap. I've just been looking for you. I should have tried your room first."

"It's okay. Why don't you come up? I just got back from a jog. I found some great spots that I sketched and if you have some time, I'd like to show them to you."

He'd been jogging. She hadn't jogged this morning in case he'd needed her. "Sure. I'll be right there."

So, he'd made progress. That was a good thing. The sooner he was done, the quicker she could advertise; maybe with luck, the place would fill up during the slow season and help pay for the air conditioning. He hadn't sketched at all yesterday but now he'd said he made sketches. Did that mean he hadn't really been inspired by the waterfall? Then again, they'd been talking so much that he hadn't really had a chance to pull out a sketchpad.

They'd given him a suite on the top floor of the resort. It was spacious, with windows that overlooked the bay. She wondered whether the view of the blue water and the sailboats had inspired him like it always did her. She liked the blue waters and the dock down the beach where the boats sat. Sailing was a big thing around the island.

She reached the fourth floor and walked down the hallway to his suite. Butterflies fluttered in her stomach as she knocked on his door. Almost before she finished, it opened and there stood Grant…in nothing but jogging shorts and a towel draped around his neck.

CHAPTER SEVEN

Cali's jaw dropped and she couldn't speak as she found her eyes locked on his damp chest. Muscled and defined, that chest made it apparent that though he was an artist, the man worked out. Of course, her brother Cam was a lean, powerful guy from all his work on the ranch so why was she surprised by Grant's muscles?

*Lean, mean working machine...*the old quote echoed in her mind—or was it fighting machine...he wasn't a fighter or mean so it didn't fit, so why was she even thinking this? She shook herself and forced her gaze off his lean, strong marvelous chest and up to meet his penetrating, blue gaze.

"Good morning." He gave her a perfect smile as he rubbed his damp hair with one side of the towel. "Sorry, I was just about to get in the shower when you called."

"Morning," she squeaked. "You stay in shape." The statement was out before she could pull it back.

"I try." His dazzling smile widened and he stepped aside so she could enter the room. "Come in."

She'd seen a million men without their shirts on— okay, maybe not a million but she'd lived on a beach and had seen a bunch. Men went shirtless as a lifestyle on the island, so why was she feeling as if his was the only chest that mattered? That stood out? That— She inhaled and forced her thoughts from his perfect torso to his face and prayed she wasn't as pink as Shar was always telling her she was around him.

No, she was probably as red as a Red Hots candy because she sure needed a cool breeze to blow in right now.

"I'll just be a few minutes. Come in and make yourself at home. This room is fantastic, by the way." He led the way toward the wide windows. The dining table was to the side and he had laid out some drawings. "Take a look at those while I'm gone and see if anything strikes your fancy." He shot her a grin and then detoured into the bedroom, closing the door behind him.

Cali breathed a sigh of relief and fought the urge to fan herself. "*You* strike my fancy," she muttered as she turned away from the closed door to stare at the table. She was in so much trouble. Little over twenty-four hours and she was a gone girl. Unable to hold off, she fanned her hot cheeks as she walked to the table. What she saw had her gasping.

There were drawings of the waterfall, and of the cliff with the old lighthouse gleaming. She picked up the sketch and was mesmerized by the beauty of the drawing. Glancing down at the others, a sketch partly hidden beneath another drawing caught her eye. Was that a wisp of long hair? She slowly drew the sketch free from the others.

She stared at herself. Her breath caught at the detail.

The breeze was blowing her hair away from her face as she looked toward the gorgeous waterfall in front of her.

He'd not drawn yesterday while they were together, but somehow he'd captured every detail on this paper. It was more than a little intimidating. It was amazing. Truly amazing.

How had he gotten every facet of her so right without at least a photo to copy?

The way he'd drawn her tugged at her gut and a longing deep inside her. There was a determination in her jaw, a gleam of excitement in her eyes, and there was peace too.

A lump formed in her throat. He'd captured a gleam of something she hadn't felt in a very long time and something she never thought she'd feel again. All three emotions had felt lost to her for good. How had he looked past the dulled expressions of the way she felt since marrying Paul and seen what she'd once looked, or at least felt, like? Or had she ever truly looked that way?

She placed the drawings on the table, strode to the sliding glass door and slipped out onto the balcony. A tear rolled from the corner of her eye. She brushed it away and stared out across Windswept Bay. Her heart clutched as more tears gathered in her eyes. *Go away.* She willed the tears to go away, but to her horror, more slipped down her cheek as she thought of the person that picture depicted…so long lost. The woman she'd lost in the last few years. The one she feared she'd never find again.

She wiped at her eyes and yet the tears continued to flow slowly down her cheeks. She dabbed them with the corner of her shirt and sniffed.

"Cali, are you all right?"

Quickly, she swiped at the tears with trembling fingertips. No one—not her sisters, her parents, or her best friends—had seen her cry since she'd come back to the bay. She was determined they wouldn't. But as she shook her head and remained facing the water, she knew that she couldn't hide the tears from Grant.

And she was right. He was behind her instantly; his strong hands cupped her shoulders as he turned her to face him. His expression clouded with concern. Of course, a tear she'd missed rolled down her cheek. Instantly, he pulled her into his arms and held her tightly; it felt so wonderful she wanted to cry harder.

"Why are you crying? What happened?"

She couldn't speak at first, she was so overwhelmed by everything. The fresh showered scent of soap and shaving cream enveloped her and her knees went weak. Her heart pounded against his and she was overwhelmed by him. By the picture, by everything.

He gently rubbed her back. "Take your time," he urged.

"You sketched me," she finally managed.

"And that made you cry?" He leaned back; his intense eyes blazed. "I'm sorry. You told me not to but I didn't know it would make you cry."

Despite her distress, a laugh escaped. She was so embarrassed that he'd caught her crying and on top of that, she was in his arms. *Dear goodness, but it was amazing.* She couldn't think straight with the feel of his strong arms around her. And the feel of his chest against hers. "It's not what you think. I loved all of your drawings. I…you just captured something in my expression that I thought I'd lost. Did you just draw that or did you see that?"

She needed to know the answer to her question.

Had he simply been drawing and that was the way it came out…not really anything she was portraying, just the slight of his hands and meaningless? Or had there been more to it—had he somehow looked at her and seen what she couldn't see any longer?

"I drew you as I saw you. As I captured you in my mind's eye in that moment in time. The way you looked was burned into my memory."

Her heart caught at his words and she tilted her face to look up at him.

He lifted a hand and with the pad of his finger, he gently wiped the tears from her cheeks. "Don't cry, Cali. I feel like you've been massively hurt and you're afraid to let it go. But yesterday, in the Jeep and at the falls, something sprang out of you that I don't even think you knew was there."

Hope hammered through her. He'd seen it, seen her the way she'd once been, and he'd captured it on paper so that she could see it. Feel it.

She wanted desperately to touch his cheek. To run the pad of her finger across his lips and then to feel those lips capture hers.

Her stomach felt bottomless as the thought sent warmth through her entire body. His eyes darkened and his hands tightened on her back as he tugged her closer.

She felt his strong body tense against her and, unable to help herself, she let her hand move to his jaw. He was going to kiss her.

He dipped his head and then brushed a kiss against her temple. "Cali, you're a gorgeous woman. But, you've been through a lot."

Yes, she had. Her good sense came back with a jolt. She stepped away from him. Her hand went to her earlobe and she tugged on it as she turned away and grasped the railing. "I'm sorry. I don't know what came over me."

"You're all right. No problems on my end of the deal. I could hold you all day and all…" He let his words drift away.

Cali knew instinctively that he'd almost said "all night."

She needed a subject change. "How did you remember those places and me with such detail?"

"I have a photographic memory when it comes to

things I like. Almost like an internal camera."

She was glad of the new topic. It was highly fascinating to her and gave her time to step outside her emotions and focus on him. Getting back to a professional relationship was what she needed. Gaining that distance but appreciation for his work was where she needed to be. Not falling all over him, thinking about kisses and more.

Both of which were totally not professional.

"That is amazing. Have you always been able to do that?"

He nodded. "I have. I might not be able to recall every conversation that I've had in my life or every page of a book, though I can get close. But I can remember everything in a room after being there momentarily or scenery but only if it captures my creative mind. It's been very useful in my line of work."

She'd captured his creative mind.

The knowledge curled warmly inside her and touched a dark corner of her heart.

"That's crazy impressive," she managed, glad to sound almost normal.

He chuckled. "It's a gift the good Lord gave me—I can't take any credit for it. It was there when I was born. But since the crash, I haven't felt inspired creatively by anything."

"I'm so sorry. But I'm so glad you feel inspired now."

"Me too."

The moment lingered between them. She started thinking about being back in his arms, but when Shar got in Cali's head and started chanting for her to kiss him, Cali knew she had to get past the moment. "I guess you're right. On that trait, you were born with it. But on your talent as an artist, did you immediately begin to paint extraordinarily perfect?" She took a step away from him.

"On that I'll have to say it was a gift, but it was one that I had to hone. I picked up a brush in college during an extracurricular art class that at the time was the only option I had in the time slot. I was hooked with the first stroke. It wasn't that good, but the feel of it when I brushed that yellow on the canvas and realized I could create something…" He gave a cute nod. "That was gold. I could see on the canvas what I wanted to be there and I began getting my vision onto the canvas."

"So the first one wasn't beautiful? I almost can't believe that."

"It was completely a beginner's work but that didn't discourage me. I felt in my soul that I could do better. And I was having fun. So I began honing my craft on Texas landscapes and horses and loved it. But the first time I painted an ocean scene on canvas, it felt right."

"I love all of your work." She made the statement with complete truth. She did.

The fact that Cam happened to be his neighbor was a fluke. She'd been a fan before he'd bought the land beside Cam's.

"Which of the drawings are you going to create for the resort?"

He turned and headed inside and picked up a drawing. "This one for the lobby." It was the waterfall but from the perspective of being beneath the water, looking up at the falls. There was an array of fish drawn in the water. "If you approve. I know you had something else in mind."

She moved to the doorway, studying the sketch. She had only thought her idea was good. This was different. Full of his signature wonder. "I love it."

A smile touched his lips. "You sure you trust me on this?"

"I do. What about the others?"

"Not there yet, unless you'll let me paint you."

"No," she said instantly.

He laughed. "That's what I thought. So how about this one instead?" He pulled out a scene that was completely underwater, of sea turtles and a colorful assortment of fish. "It's a simple scene but for the pool area it feels right. I'd like to bring the animals to the kids."

"Shar will love this. She works with the sea turtle rescue hospital here on the island."

"Then that's perfect. If we paint the turtles, that would help draw attention to the work they do."

"Perfect," she repeated. And she knew that as he always did with his paintings, he would put treasures in his paintings. Hidden things that one had to purposefully look for. Glistening sand with a crab peeking out at you that you would miss if you weren't looking to discover it.

"I'm so pleased. The children will have a blast discovering what you've hidden among the coral and rocks for them to find."

"That's what I always hope for… Look, I need to be honest with you. This is the first time I've painted since the crash. And I can't guarantee it'll be my best."

He moved past Cali and over to the railing again and stared out at the ocean. Every line in his face was tense. Cali stood beside him and suddenly wanted to smooth the lines from his brow with her fingertips…or her lips. She was losing her mind. That's all there was to it. Or Shar had come to live in her mind and that was the same thing as losing it.

"You'll be okay." She placed her hand on his. "The fact that you've struggled is a testament to how much you cared about the men who died."

"I cared. But doing something that brings me joy just doesn't feel right. I can't explain it. And until I got here and spent time with you yesterday, I wasn't sure I even found joy in it anymore. But I do. I know that at least."

She pulled her hand from his, too aware of the hum of electricity buzzing through her. "That's a start," she urged. "You'll figure it out as you go."

He nodded. "So far, anyway. I just wanted to warn you."

"I'm duly warned. I better go now, and let you get busy." She headed inside the sliding glass door.

"Is that what you're doing? Figuring it out as you go?"

She paused with one hand on the doorframe. "It is. So that's my only helpful explanation. I came back to the island, to the place and the people I love. And I'm staying busy and I'm determined to move forward." And she was.

The fact that she had an infatuation with him was nothing.

Infatuation. That was a good word.

It explained everything.

CHAPTER EIGHT

Cali headed back to work now that he planned to go ahead and begin working in the lobby as soon as he organized his supplies. Now that he'd made a decision to paint, he seemed distracted and as she left, she hoped that it was because his mind was on the work ahead of him and not the tragedy behind him.

She knew how that could be. Although, her tragedy was far different than his. Innocent men had perished in his tragic past but that couldn't be said about hers. Paul had not been innocent. And he was still alive and well last time she'd heard anything. It was one of the sad, unfair things about life. Good men often died and sorry ones remained. And only God knew why.

She had no plans to let thoughts of her ex sidetrack her today, so she shoved him under the proverbial rug and instead of leaving thoughts of him there as usual, this time she gave the rug a good hard kick for good measure.

And then she moved on as the memory of the sketch Grant had drawn of her made her smile. She couldn't explain it but it felt good that he'd seen that determination and strength in her. Even when she hadn't felt it.

"Now that's more like it," Horace said when she walked off the elevator. "Got a smile on those pretty lips and a pep in your step."

She placed her hands on her hips and cocked her head up to where he was working on another light fixture. "Are you sure you're working or just perched up there watching everyone and giving out hard times?"

"I'm working. And giving a hard time to anyone I can."

"That's what I thought."

"Hey, keeps life interesting. I do like to people watch and I'm wondering what happened on the top floor to put that smile on your face? Wouldn't be our painter, would it?"

Nothing got by the man. She wasn't exactly sure how he knew she'd been on the top floor but she wasn't going to deny it. "Mr. Ellington is going to begin working on the lobby mural tomorrow, I think. He may start organizing his things this afternoon. Or this evening. If your crew could move the furniture out of his way that would be helpful."

"You got it, boss. Grant told me when he came in from his jog he was probably going to work this afternoon."

She sighed. Of course Horace already knew; why had she even thought he might not? "Right, then you've got it handled. You're a gem and you know it."

He chuckled. "I'm just a plain old rock that aims to please."

"If you say so. See you later."

"Don't forget about the air conditioner," he called.

She waved over her shoulder as she headed back up the stairs. "Oh believe me, I won't." With thoughts of Grant very nearly kissing her, a heavy-duty new air conditioning system would be nice because right now the one they had was not doing its job. She was about to burn up.

As luck would have it, the office was empty and she was able to finish her work for the afternoon in peace. Thoughts of Grant played havoc enough on her concentration without having to worry with her sisters. By four, she was caught up and decided to call it an early day. Everyone had her number and knew to reach her on that if she was needed. And if she left now, she could avoid seeing Jillian or Shar at all again today and put off her inquisition a little longer.

Heading down the back hallway and out the private exit, she had to fight the urge to peek into the lobby and see whether Grant had started to set up his work station. She didn't, though. She had had him on her mind too much and she needed space.

It was a small wall when compared to other walls that he'd painted but for Grant it felt as though it were a mile high and a mile wide as he worked. He couldn't explain it; though he knew Mike, the young pilot and David, his friend wouldn't begrudge him moving on, it was still hard. But this painting might help Cali. Her tears drove him. He could do this for her.

He worked in his room the rest of the afternoon, drawing out proportions of the various parts of the mural and then he went down around midnight and began to work. Horace, his new best friend, had organized his paints for him just as he'd asked him to.

The lobby was quiet at midnight. The older woman manning the front desk stayed in her office most of the time, as if she sensed he wanted to be alone.

Working at midnight was a pretty good hint.

Still, the first stroke was hard. Bold, deep cerulean. He stared at it for a long moment after he'd drawn his paintbrush over the wall. He always said a prayer before he painted his paintings…not that he was going to win a Nobel Peace Prize or paint anything of real meaning in the whole scheme of life, but he did want his talents to move people. To cause them to see the intricate beauty and wonder of creation. It wasn't much, but it was what he did.

Tonight, he sent one up for Mike and David and the families they'd left behind.

And then, with hands not as steady as they usually were, he went to work.

When Cali walked into the lobby the next morning, it was with a sense of anticipation. Grant would start painting today; the very idea thrilled her. It would be hard to get any work done with the constant temptation of wanting to watch him work. She was startled to find a crowd in the lobby. It was full when she walked inside. People were everywhere and they were all watching Grant.

Cali gasped at the painting that was on the wall. "But…" was all she could get out. He stood on a ladder, Horace's ladder, and was intent on the colors he was working into the waterfall. The magnificent, alive, and practically breathing waterfall.

"He worked all night." Beth, one of the receptionists, came to stand beside Cali. "Laverne said he started about midnight and worked like a man possessed. She stayed in the office, out of his way, and watched on the video feed because she didn't want to interfere with his art."

"I thought he was going to paint today, and just prep last night. I had no idea."

Beth sighed. "I don't even know if he realizes we're all here watching him. He hasn't looked at anything but that wall and those paints."

"Thanks, Beth. Could you put my bag in the office? I think I better see if he needs anything."

"Sure. And if you need help, just call and I'll come running."

Cali handed her bag over and then made her way through the group of guests. She reached the bottom of the ladder and looked up. "Grant, hey. It's gorgeous. Amazing. Is there anything I can do to help?"

He didn't acknowledge her at first but finished the reflection he was working on. Then he looked down at her; her heart clamored at the intensity glowing in those eyes so blue even the ocean couldn't compete.

"Cali, you should be sleeping."

She laughed. "It's eight a.m. You're the one who should be sleeping." He looked weary, deeply drawn, but there was no denying the vitality in his eyes, in every move he made. He had said when he painted he had a one-track mind but she hadn't expected this. "Are you okay?"

"Yes. Nearly finished." He came down the ladder and placed his brush in a container. "I'll sleep when I'm done. I've hit my stride and can't stop. Black coffee would be good, though."

"I'll get it," a young woman called; she rushed from the crowd and bolted toward the coffee shop at the end of the lobby.

It was crazy but he looked startled to see everyone. When they all started clapping, Cali could have sworn it just registered to him that they were all there. "Thank you," he said, gruffly. "I didn't mean to ignore you. Come back later and it'll be finished."

"Got it! Here's your coffee." The young woman

rushed back through the crowd. She couldn't be more than eighteen. "It's black, just like you asked."

Cali could not blame the girl for her adoration.

"Thank you." Grant dug in his pocket and pulled out some dollars.

"Oh no, I don't want your money." The girl held up her hands and backed away. "I'd pay to watch you paint." She sighed and then brightened, glancing at Cali. "Could you take our picture?"

Cali could see Grant was struggling not to climb back on the ladder. "Sure, and then maybe you could go to the pool and come back later to see the finished product."

"Sure." She sidled up next to Grant and smiled as if he'd just asked her to marry him. Cali snapped the shot with the girls smartphone and hoped Grant wasn't frowning too big in the photo. The girl grabbed her phone and headed off, staring at it as though it were gold. Total and complete fan girl.

Cali wasn't that bad—at least, she hoped.

"Does that happen often?"

"Often enough." He frowned and took a drink of

the coffee and then sat it on the makeshift table beside his paint. "I need to get back. I'll talk later."

And then he climbed back up the ladder with a new paintbrush loaded with fresh paint and closed out the world around him.

One-track mind, he'd said that first day.

That was a steel vault he had there when he picked up a paintbrush.

When Grant finished painting, he was exhausted. Once he'd started, it was as if everything he had in him came out on the canvas…or wall, considering that was his canvas of choice. Both anticipation and sorrow swirled inside him as he'd worked. And in the end, it was just the work that mattered. The painting itself drew him, took everything he had to give and for the while that he painted, everything else slipped away. When he was finished, though, the adrenaline shut down and he paid the toll.

Cali, who'd not intruded but must have stayed near, appeared as he headed toward the elevators. He could hardly hold his eyes open.

"Grant?" she asked.

He handed her the paintbrush he still had in his hand. "Later."

"I'll close up your paint," Horace said, also appearing from somewhere.

Grant nodded and then walked to the open elevator doors and punched the button for the fourth floor. Adrenaline had seen him through but now every limb ached. His arms felt like lead weights. When he reached his room, he peeled his shirt off before he sat on the edge of the bed. He reached for the snap on his shorts but closed his eyes for a moment and then fell against the covers.

This happened sometimes, when the work flowed like lava in a slow, burning rush that couldn't be stopped. But never had it taken everything he had.

He closed his eyes and slept.

CHAPTER NINE

Cali wasn't sure what to do. When Grant had handed her the paintbrush and walked past her, he'd looked drained. She wasn't sure whether this was normal for him or not. It wasn't normal at all but then, she'd never been around an artist and maybe it was normal.

But, again, it wasn't normal to her. And she was completely not making sense as she thought about how he'd looked. How he'd acted. All she knew was that she was concerned. And she needed to make sure he was okay.

Shar walked over and plucked the paintbrush from her hand. "That wasn't normal."

Leave it to Shar to say what she was thinking. "No. You're right—it wasn't."

"I'll clean this up. You need to go check on him. He looked like he'd been up for days when he walked by here. And Cali, he looked like he was in pain."

"Yes, he did," Jillian agreed, coming down the stairs to where they stood. "Here, go check on him. I grabbed the master key in case you need it." She pushed it into Cali's hand.

"Wait, why me?"

"Oh please." Shar glared at her. "You should see yourself in the mirror. You're worried sick and you know good and well why it's you who needs to check on the man."

"Fine," she growled and headed for the elevator. She wasn't sure what Shar thought she saw in her expression but it was simply concern. That was all.

When she reached the fourth floor, she walked to his door and knocked lightly. There was no answer. Maybe he was in the shower. Unable to help herself, needing to make sure he hadn't passed out on the floor from exhaustion, she used the key and slipped inside. The first thing she saw was his shirt on the floor. She hesitated, her heart thundering. She should go. But, she had to make sure he was in bed and not sprawled on the floor passed out.

"Grant," she called softly. There was no sound, so she peeked into the room. He lay flat on his back, his feet still touching the floor.

Aw... Something she didn't want to think too hard about curled inside her and, unable to stop herself, she leaned down and tenderly brushed a dark curl from his forehead. She stayed there, peering down at him. Even in sleep, weariness remained etched around his eyes and pulled at the edges of his lips. She wondered whether sleep was hard for him since the plane crash that cost him his friends. Wondered how much he hurt inside where no one could see. She reached to touch him but yanked her hand back just in time, rubbing her fingers on her thigh instead of along the sun-etched lines at the edges of his eyes. His beautiful eyes.

With a jerk, she stepped back. She needed to leave.

He was breathing easy, calmly, peacefully. Exactly what he needed right now.

She needed to leave.

Swallowing hard, she stepped back another step and then remembered his feet were still touching the floor. She couldn't leave him like that. She touched her temple, tapped it as if checking to see whether she had a brain. Proving she didn't, she knelt and grasped his ankle and then eased his Nikes off. He sighed and her stomach dipped. Hurrying, she removed the other. He grunted; she glanced at him, not wanting to wake him now to find her kneeling at the edge of his bed!

Tempted to duck and crawl away, she realized if he woke that would be even more weird so she shot to her feet.

Leave now.

But no. Instead, she reached across him, grasped the coverlet and pulled it across him. His hand moved and covered hers. Her gaze locked onto his, but he was still sleeping. She could barely breathe, much less think, as his fingers curled around her hand and drew up to his cheek as he rolled to his side, facing away from her. The move had her twisting over him awkwardly, with her hand trapped blissfully against his cheek.

Groaning, she closed her eyes and as easily as she could, she tugged her fingers from his and ran.

She didn't turn around until she was on the elevator and pushing the down button.

Grant rolled over and rubbed his eyes as sunlight assaulted them. His head pounded. Sitting up, he looked around and for a moment, forgot where he was. *Cali.*

The painting.

He rubbed a hand down his face as bits came back in a rush. Everyone probably thought he was crazy. He was starving.

He glanced at the clock. It was three in the afternoon. But what afternoon?

His phone buzzed in his pocket and he reached for it. He saw Cam's ID and answered. "Hey," he said, his voice still gruff with sleep.

"Are you alive?"

"Yeah, I am. Starting to come back now."

"Well, that's a good thing since you have my sister worried sick."

"Sorry about that. This was a tough one. But, Cam, it's good." He felt light, and knew he'd done right by Cali and her resort. The mural was one of his best. In the waters of that waterfall, he'd given his all. Finding Cali crying on his balcony the day he'd shown her the drawings had been like an arrow to his heart. He'd wanted to kiss her, to hold her and wipe those blasted tears away for good. But all he'd known at that moment that he could really do for her was give her the paintings she wanted so badly. And that was what he was doing.

When he'd escorted her to his door, he'd been distracted by all the emotions she caused in him when she was near. The tears had just upped the stakes.

"Yeah, Cali told me it was unbelievable." Cam cut into Grant's thoughts. "She's worried about you, though. You've been asleep for more than twenty-four hours. Is that normal?"

"No, not exactly. But since I haven't had a good night of sleep since the plane went down and I worked nonstop on the mural, I guess it is this time. I need a shower and food. I'm sorry I worried everyone. Cali?"

"Yeah, man. Cali has called me twice, wanting me to call you. I finally decided maybe I better. Glad to have you back in the world of the living. Hopefully in more ways than one. Get a shower. I'll call Cali."

"Thanks." *She was worried about him.* That was a good thing.

He hung up and headed toward the shower. He'd dreamed Cali had tucked him in and caressed his cheek. It felt real.

It felt right.

"Is he alive up there?"

Cali nibbled on the inside of her cheek and stared at Shar. "Of course he is."

"It's nearly three and no one, other than you, has seen him since he handed you his paintbrush yesterday at one."

"I called Cam again. I am not going back to his room. He needs sleep. He was wiped out. I think it had something to do with the stress of the plane crash and the stress of not being sure he had another painting inside him. He needs sleep. He looked worn-out, even when he was sleeping."

Shar frowned. "Okay, but I need to go to the hospital and help. Let me know when Sleeping Beauty wakes up."

"I will."

Jillian watched their sister leave and then turned back to Cali. "I bet you're right. Maybe he's been sleepless and depressed, at least to some degree, since the plane crash. Maybe this helped him."

Cali wasn't sure she'd classify it as depression, but it could be. He was alive and his friends were dead and the tragedy had left a toll on him that not everyone could see.

She hoped knowing he could still paint would help him.

Sleep had evaded her last night. Thoughts of him had kept her awake and curled up with a blanket on her porch swing.

There was a quick knock on the door and Grant looked around the corner. "Well, I'm alive."

Jillian jumped up and hurried to him. "You scared us. Come in. How are you? You must be starved."

"I'm famished, actually, and alive. I thought I'd see if your sister would ride with me to eat somewhere."

Cali stood and smiled. "Hey," she said, barely above a whisper. "You are alive."

"I am. Now, about that food?"

"She'll go." Jillian hitched a brow at her.

"Sure I will. Of course." She glanced at her watch. "I only have an hour. I have a meeting with a wedding party."

Jillian frowned and glanced down at her jeans that were smudged with their usual dirt. "I'm not exactly dressed for a meeting like that or I'd take it over for you."

"I can eat a lot in an hour."

Cali laughed. "Okay then, so let's go feed you, you painting machine. I just hope one of your fans doesn't knock me over to get a selfie with you."

"It'll be fine. I'm not that memorable when I'm not standing in front of one of my murals with a paintbrush in my hand."

"Yeah, tell that to coffee girl. She'd know you anywhere."

Turned out, Cali was right. They ended up at a beachside restaurant, eating between him taking photos with dozens of people who'd watched him paint the lobby mural.

When they finally made it out of the patio porch she reluctantly headed back to her office. She'd enjoyed watching Grant interact with those who admired him. She admired him too, and knew that she'd be distracted for the rest of the afternoon with him on her mind.

Grant watched her leave. He was in the deep end of the pool—he'd almost kissed her two days ago when she'd been crying on his balcony. He'd come fully awake in the shower earlier and everything had flooded back. He'd been undone by the strong emotions when he found her crying. It had broken his heart.

She'd been crying silently, alone, and he was determined to find out why. How bad had her divorce been? Did she still care for the guy? That didn't ring true from what little Cam had said and what she'd said so far. So why?

Had he done something to her? The picture of her had triggered something…why?

The desire to wipe the tears from her eyes and fill them with joy was overwhelming. He wanted to see that carefree woman who jumped into her Jeep that first day and tore out of the parking lot. The one who'd looked at him with a gleam of challenge in her eyes that he wasn't even sure she'd known was there. And again, he wondered why. Was it something to do with the divorce?

If so, he planned to find out.

CHAPTER TEN

He called her that night while he sat on the beach, watching the waves roll in. He felt edgy and alone and he just wanted to hear her voice.

"Hey, it's me," he said, when she answered.

"Hi. Is everything all right?"

That was a loaded question he decided to sidestep. "I'm going to pick up supplies in the morning. Can you come with me? And mark some time off on your schedule?"

She hesitated. "Of course," she said at last. "I hope you had a good afternoon."

"I did. I'll show you tomorrow. Sleep good."

"You too."

Short and sweet—that was all he trusted himself with at the moment. But he had a date.

And hopefully by morning he'd have his head screwed on a little straighter.

Boy, that was a joke, he thought the next morning. One look at her in her sundress and barely there flip-flops and any progress he'd made went out the window. But he had a lot to show her and he focused on that and not how pretty her legs looked in that soft yellow dress.

He hadn't told her last night how good an afternoon he'd had but it had been good.

"Where are you going?" she asked when they reached the parking lot and she headed toward her Jeep and he went in the opposite direction.

He grinned. "I have wheels today. I decided relying solely on the kindness of others while I was here wasn't fitting me, so Horace took me to see his friend Charlie, who owns Charlie's Used Cars and Rentals, and I bought a Jeep of my own."

"You did not." She gasped.

He laughed at her disbelief. "I did. And why do you look so shocked?"

"Charlie's is a rent-a-wreck place."

"Now, don't go calling my Jeep names before you've seen her."

"Her, huh? Let me find her." She scanned the lot and immediately stopped on the twenty-year-old, faded, light-blue Jeep with one white front fender and an unpainted patch on the rear fender. If that wasn't enough to set it apart, it also had jacked up off-road tires that were made for exploring. A bubble of laughter spontaneously escaped Cali and she pointed. "An educated guess."

"Don't laugh. She may look less than gorgeous but boy can she crawl over rock crevices. Come on, hop in."

"Hop being the literal term here," Cali drawled, staring at the seat that was about chest high.

"Do you need me to give you a lift?" He moved to stand beside her and shot her a grin. To his joy, she gave him a cute look of scorn and then grabbed the roll bar. Just before she climbed into the seat, she frowned. "Maybe you need to look the other way. I was not intending to climb Pikes Peak today in this sundress."

He glanced at the dress that hit her about mid-thigh. "Yup, I see what you mean. I can put you up there—"

"I can do it. Turn, please."

He sighed and looked away.

"Okay, you can hop in."

She sat in the passenger seat, her skirt flirting dangerously high on her thighs.

"That was quick." He jogged around and climbed behind the wheel. He grinned at her, feeling more uplifted than he'd been in months. And it felt good.

As they drove along the beach road and into town, Cali felt that same sense of exhilaration sitting beside Grant that she'd felt from almost the first moment of meeting him. She loved that he'd bought such a road-worn Jeep to travel around on the island. He had the means to have bought a brand-new Jeep and then resell it for a loss if he'd been inclined to. But no, he'd bought one of Charlie's cheap rent-a-wrecks. And the result was that he looked perfectly at home on the island now. He fit in as if he'd been here forever. He wore an old straw cowboy hat that shaded his eyes and reminded her of a country music video of Kenny Chesney riding around on an island in a topless Jeep. Like Kenny, fitting in with island life when he liked to relax, Grant seemed to do the same.

"You seem really relaxed and happy this morning," she said as the salty breeze kissed her skin and streamed through her hair as they rode down the narrow road.

"I am. This island is beautiful. I'm glad I came. I did a little exploring yesterday. Getting the first painting done was a good thing.

"How are you? We haven't talked much really since the day you were on my balcony."

She didn't want to go there right now. "I'm fine. Let's not go there right now."

"You were crying."

And you nearly kissed me. "You captured something that touched me. That's it. I'm a girl. Girls cry."

"We're going to talk about it." He pulled into the parking lot of the kayak rental business located beside a lagoon. It was a popular place for tourists.

"Really, Grant. I don't want to. And especially not here in this busy parking lot."

"Oh, no, we'll talk later, but we will talk. This is what I want to show you."

He climbed out of the Jeep and though she was confused as to why they were here, she followed him.

"What are we doing here?" She went to stand beside him on the boardwalk leading along the side of the building around to the back where the entrance and lagoon access was.

"We're going for a ride."

It had been a long time but she'd been down the lagoon many times growing up. It wove through the Windswept Bay interior and to the ocean. "But I thought you had found something to paint?"

"I have, but I'm still looking for what will be the best. Earlier today, I was talking to Jax, the owner of Lagoon Adventures, and he piqued my interest. He told me of some cool places the lagoon runs past."

She'd been having fun but now she looked down at her dress and then back at him. "I'm not exactly dressed for kayaking. You could have asked me if I wanted to do this."

He looked shamefaced. "I was afraid you'd say no."

"I can still say no," she pointed out, feeling her irritation evaporating when he grinned at her. The man was too appealing.

"Yes you can, but I'm hoping you won't. I promise."

He held out his hand to her. She told herself that he would be leaving and that for now she could just enjoy being around him while he was here. That he would leave and she'd have used him as a trial for moving into a new segment of her life. Shar and Jillian were right; she did need to move forward. And Grant was an amazing man, with an amazing career, and knowing he would leave was like a…a safety net of sorts.

Life was full of risks. She could do this.

She slipped her hand in his. "Let's have another adventure."

"That's my girl." He winked at her.

Suddenly she wasn't sure whether she'd just made a mistake. Being his girl sounded far too perfect.

They headed to the outside window, where a young man waited. "You came back," he said to Grant.

"I told you you'd given me a great idea yesterday. I just needed to bring my friend. Do you know each other?"

The young man was sandy-haired and had the look of a surfer. He looked slightly familiar to her but Cali didn't know him. "I don't think we've met but you do look familiar. I'm Cali Sinclair."

His green eyes lit up. "You own the resort. My girl works there. I'm Jax, by the way." He held out his hand and she shook it.

"Who is your girlfriend?"

"Blair Baines. She works with your sister in the gardens. She loves it."

This was a part of being back that Cali loved. Knowing they were supplying jobs for the islanders and that they were enjoying those jobs made her feel good. Knowing that they could make it even better pushed her to work harder. "If she's working with Jillian, then Blair is learning from the best."

"She says the same thing. So, you two ready to take

a ride on the lagoon?"

"We're ready," Grant said. "I want to show Cali something around the building. We'll be right back."

"Sure thing."

The look in Grant's eyes caused anticipation to fill her. The man was always causing something like that to happen. He took her hand and led her toward the end of the building. "This place is cool. It not only has lagoon access but also on the backside it has beach access." He turned the corner and she saw the beach down the sloping hill.

When they rounded the corner, Cali gasped when she saw the gorgeous mural on the wall. It was of a large wave; a surfer was in the tunnel and several others were watching it from the water. But it was the various blue hues of the water that was spectacular. Not Grant Ellington spectacular but it was wonderful.

"It's wonderful." She repeated what she'd thought. Walking over, she touched it. "This reminds me of your work."

"I thought so too. I was jogging down the beach yesterday evening when I spotted it. The kid painted it."

"Oh wow. Did you ask him about it?"

"No, I wanted you to see it first. You brought me here to paint something amazing and it looks to me like you've got the talent right on the island."

She looked at him sharply. "Are you wanting out?"

His eyes crinkled at the edges. "No, but I would like to ask you if you'd mind if I asked Jax to help with the painting. I hate to see his talent not be recognized."

His proposal stunned her. "You'd do that?"

"I need some help on the big project, if I can get it, and I like to encourage people to use their talent."

She loved the idea. "Sure, ask him. I can't believe I hadn't seen this. But I've been away for several years."

They walked back around the building and waited on Jax to get another couple into their kayak. After they had paddles in hand and were moving down the lagoon, he turned back to them, running a hand through his shoulder-length hair.

"Ready?"

Grant nodded. "First I'd like to talk about the stunning mural on this building that you painted."

"Sure." He shrugged. "And thanks, I just tried it.

But it's not the best. It's not an Ellington."

Grant laughed. "Well, it's close. Maybe a little crude in a few areas and maybe not the right technique to preserve it for years, but for the wood you painted it on, it's great."

Questions filled Jax's eyes. "Man, you sound like you know what you're talking about."

Cali smiled. "He does."

Grant still didn't say his name and Cali realized that with his cap and shades, even someone who knew what he looked like might not recognize him. "You have talent, Jax. Did you take lessons?"

He shrugged. "Nah, no money for that. I just saw a great picture of a building online and it got me in the gut and I decided to try it."

Grant laughed, a big, robust laugh that made her chuckle and goose bumps to shiver across her skin. It was obvious Grant was having a great time with this.

"You are amazing, Jax. Do you know how much talent it takes to pick up a brush and paint something like that? Your scale is great. Your eye is good. You should pursue it."

"Thanks, man. But, it's not like doing that is going to pay my bills or anything. I'm into making a living. I plan to ask Blair to marry me soon and this business pays my bills."

Cali couldn't take it any longer. "Jax, this is Grant Ellington and he loves your work."

Jax looked startled and then squinted; she saw recognition dawn.

"Holy smokes, it is you."

"It's good to meet you, Jax. And I've got to tell you that if my work inspired you to pick up a brush, then I'm pumped by that."

"Wow, man. You're excellent."

"You're excellent. You could be better than me if you took to it."

Jax looked at them in disbelief. "You're really serious, aren't you?"

"Oh, I am without doubt. And I'd like to make you a proposition. I'm here, about ready to paint a couple of murals at the resort. I need an assistant. I'd pay you and you'd get some experience."

"Seriously?"

The kid liked that word.

Grant nodded. "Why don't you come by tomorrow and we'll talk after I show you what we'd be up against."

"Sure, man. I've got to at least hear you out."

"Sounds like a plan. Now we'll head out and see what magic waits for us down the lagoon."

Jax grinned. "Have fun. I still can't believe you're here."

"One day someone could be saying the same thing about you."

Cali loved it. She took Grant's hand and cautiously got into the front seat of the two-seater kayak. With her skirt, it took some maneuvering not to embarrass herself but in the end she made it without flipping the kayak and dumping herself into the water. Within a few minutes, they were headed down the lagoon. The green foliage was a canopy above their heads and the sounds of the forest once again took over around them. And the peacefulness surrounded them.

But she was far from peaceful. Grant had just shown her another side of him and the man just kept getting better and better. But she was touched by the fact that he didn't just act humble; he was. "Are you going to give Jax a credit for working on the murals?"

"Of course. He'll learn a lot on these projects. And if he's as good as it looks like he is, then he can gain some great recognition. Don't get me wrong, I'm glad to be doing this project for you but the thought of helping a guy out who has absolutely no idea how good he is is cool."

"You love giving back."

"I do. Paying it forward with an overlooked artist makes me happy. Jax is the perfect example of someone who is underutilizing his talent. And, this means a lot to me."

She knew he was thinking about the men who'd died. "I can understand that. Artists come from all over to paint here. I think it's a wonderful idea."

They let the lagoon take them along then, and for a little while they were quiet. It dawned on Cali that it had been a very long time since she just relaxed. Hiking to the falls had been beautiful but it had been a hike. This was effortless. Yes, they were in a kayak with paddles but the lagoon was doing the work.

The only problem that she could see with the situation was that when the lagoon did the work, that left more time for her to think. And she was thinking about the intriguing man sitting behind her.

CHAPTER ELEVEN

"So, how does it feel to be a part of such a large family?" Grant knew that Cali's family was huge and he needed something to talk about. Sitting behind her in the kayak, he found his attention constantly on her russet curls and the graceful movements of her arms as she dipped her paddle into the water. She was no stranger to kayaking but that wasn't what his mind kept getting stuck on… He kept thinking about how she'd felt in his arms. He kept thinking about everything about her.

He needed something to talk about and he wanted

to know more about her, so asking about her family seemed a good subject. She paused paddling and glanced over her shoulder. She had a face he could look at endlessly.

"It's great and overwhelming at the same time. Can you imagine being a girl and growing up with five brothers? It was interesting to say the least. My only saving grace was that I had three sisters."

He laughed. "I see your point. Then again, I see your brothers' point too."

"You would." She chuckled. "On top of that, as you've seen since you've been here, my sisters are a bit nosey. That is not something new. Being the older sister with triplets as sisters has been interesting to say the least. I've often felt like their own personal test subject guinea pig." She laughed and it said a lot.

"I've seen two of them in action. It must have been interesting growing up with three mischievous younger sisters." He could hear the affection in her voice and the love. He imagined that she'd been a great big sister to the little gang of girls.

"Ah, you'd be right about that." Cali dipped the

paddle into the water and matched Grant's rhythm. The words were out before she thought better of them.

"So they're doing some matchmaking?"

She looked back at him, shocked. "No—" The quirk of his eyebrow halted her denial. "Maybe. Sorry, but so you know, it's harmless. I'm not interested." She wasn't. Infatuated yes, but not interested.

His expression was almost comical at those words. "Well, thank you."

"No, I meant…" *How could she have been so careless?* "That wasn't about you. It was about me."

A seagull cried in the air above them, signaling they were getting closer to the opening of the river into the ocean. Her gaze was caught by Grant's and she couldn't look away.

"It's about me, too. And you are interested."

She blinked but still couldn't tear her eyes away from the direct look in his. She swallowed hard. *How was she supposed to answer that?* "True," she said at last. "But I won't let myself act on it and you should know that. No matter how hard my sisters push."

"Is it because of your divorce?"

She nodded. "So you should be warned."

The glint in his eyes sent a buzz through her. She got the uneasy feeling that her words had fallen on deaf ears.

Grant had not known how Cali would feel about the day. He'd had to bring her, had to show her what he'd seen and he knew that there was no way he was going to walk away from the emotions that she was bringing to him. With her, he had been able to step away from the thoughts of the crash that rode on his shoulders constantly. He was starting to see his way again and it felt good. The survivor's guilt was still there but he was dealing better with it. Cali made him feel as though there were a light at the end of the dark tunnel.

They guided the kayak from the lagoon out into the calm bay. They were lucky enough for a pair of porpoises to come swim beside them. Their slick gray bodies gleamed in the sun as they leapt from the waters, arching as they dove back into the waves in perfect time together.

"I never get tired of seeing them do that," Cali called over her shoulder, shooting him a bright smile that was alive and joyful.

"Me either," he called, loving her smile.

By the time they got out of the kayak back at Lagoon Adventures, Grant had scenes of Cali and the dolphins dancing in his mind's eye. The joyful expression was one he knew most visitors felt when seeing the beautiful creatures. The problem with the murals was that he knew she wouldn't want to be the subject of the paintings she'd brought him here to paint. But so far, he knew he'd put her in every one of them if he had his way.

When they made it back to the resort, Cali had work to do and was glad of it. She needed something to keep her feet on the ground. She'd had so much fun being with Grant. And had seen more and more what a good man he was—proving the articles she'd read about him were true.

Which made keeping the attraction she felt toward

him all that much harder to hold back. She needed distance and she was thankful that today she had to meet with a couple again to go over the plans for the wedding that would be held on the beach in two weeks. Jillian would be heading up this meeting because it was about the flowers and there really wasn't that much that Cali had to do. Still, she needed to be there just in case there were last-minute detail changes.

When the couple and the bride's mother left, Cali turned to stare out the window. Her gaze snagged instantly on Grant as he started working on the pool wall.

From the glass windows of the garden room where the wedding reception would be held, she had a clear view of him. He wore taupe cargo shorts that had paint droppings on them and a light-colored shirt with dried paint on it too. It was similar to what he'd worn in the lobby when he'd painted but today there was something different about him.

He was relaxed today. Not tense and possessed as he had been working on the amazing waterfall. Word was out and people were driving from Tampa and

Naples so far to see it. And they were all planning to come back to see the final two.

He looked at home and comfortable, almost as if he belonged here on the island. Of course, he didn't and she needed to keep that in her head. She could not forget that he was leaving.

"Earth to Cali. Earth to Cali—"

The sound of her name registered. "Hmmm?" she murmured, unable to tear her eyes and her thoughts away from watching him.

"That's what I thought." Jillian stepped up beside her. The movement and her words finally drew Cali out of the near trance that had hijacked her.

"Thought what?" Cali looked at her sister curiously.

"That this is far more than just a casual attraction. You're absolutely besotted with your artist."

"He's not my artist," Cali denied. She met Jillian's knowing gaze.

"I beg to differ. Besides, I caught you staring."

Cali sighed. "You are entirely too observant. I was thinking about my morning kayaking out on the bay with Grant. It had been spontaneous and fabulous… I had forgotten what it was like to feel the breeze and sun on my face and the water beneath me."

Jillian's face lit up. "Oh, Cali, that makes me so happy. You used to love to do that. I'm glad Grant got you back out there. He's good for you."

"I've known him less than a week." *What was it—four days? Five days?* It felt as if she'd known him forever.

"So? He's still good for you."

"The man can be maddening. I wasn't even dressed for it."

"You aren't wet or dirty, so it must have worked out." A smile played at the corner of Jillian's mouth and her eyes crinkled at the edges.

"It did," Cali said, giving in to the need to talk.

"So has he kissed you yet?"

Cali's mouth dropped open. She stuttered, "Wh-what…n-no. I expect questions like that from Shar, not you."

Jillian laughed. "I can't help it. You two looked extremely combustible when you're near each other. I just thought maybe…"

"Combustible?"

"Absolutely. You're turning red all over again."

Cali had wanted Grant to kiss her so many different times on that trip that she'd been glad she was trapped in the front end of the yellow kayak. It kept her from launching herself at him. Not to mention the day he'd passed out on his bed. It was probably useless to try to deny her feelings when she felt heat roll through her every time she looked at him or thought of him. Could he see what her sisters so easily saw?

She certainly hoped not.

"Invite him to dinner at Mom and Dad's tonight. Everyone wants to meet him."

"Sure." Cali knew Jillian was right but now she had to worry that everyone in her family might see her attraction to Grant. If—when—they did, what would she do then?

CHAPTER TWELVE

Grant was almost finished applying his base coat on the wall in the pool area when his phone rang. He set the roller in the pan and pulled the phone from his pocket.

"How's it going out there in paradise now that you've gotten some sleep?"

"Better. I didn't tell you on the last call but this is a great place. Your family has a gorgeous property. I can see why it's been around for so long."

"Yeah, I miss it. I'm getting the itch to come for a visit. If I could raise and sell cattle and horses from there, I'd probably still be there full-time."

"I can understand that. I did notice when I was out driving around with Cali this morning that there was a sign to a horse farm and riding not far down the beach."

"It's a small operation. Mostly for riding on the beach. Bess, the older woman who owns the place, has had it for years. I actually learned to ride there as a kid and that's where I knew I'd grow up and own a ranch."

"I'll have to check it out while I'm here."

"You should. So, Cali and you were driving this morning? You two seem to be spending a lot of time together." Cam didn't even try to hide his interest.

"She's amazing. She's showing me the island to help me get inspiration for the murals."

"How does she seem to be doing?" Concern filled Cam's voice. "I know you're pretty observant. What do you think?"

"I think she's been hurt. She's very cautious and there's a wall up that would stop a tsunami." *But I'm making progress.*

"That's what I figured. Look, while you're there, would you look out for her? Maybe take her out to dinner. You're a good guy, Grant. And I know you've been through a lot and have your own scars to get past. But, I hadn't thought about it until now, you could show her that not all men are like that jerk that she was married to."

"I'm glad to have you in my corner for that. But there are some things that have to be overcome in their own time. I can tell you that from my own perspective. I don't talk much about it, Cam, as you know, but grief, regret—things that cut deep don't just disappear because people around you want them to get better."

Cam was silent on the other end of the line. Grant didn't want to talk about the plane crash but he felt he could give Cam an insight into what Cali might be going through. He would be more than happy to help in any way he could. Maybe because he and Cali did have open wounds right now, they could help each other. Or at least be a distraction from the feelings that warred constantly inside him. Maybe it was the same for Cali.

"I get it," Cam said at last. "But it doesn't hurt a big brother to want to help. I know everyone in our family is worried that there was more to her divorce than she's let on. She's been very private about it. But she's different. More closed off and it's like a light went off inside her. Shar called and said she lights up when you're around."

"Cam, there's something there but that's all I'm saying. I'm on rocky land right now and it's obvious Cali is too. So if you're joining in with your sisters on matchmaking—"

"No matchmaking for me. I'd urge caution while at the same time a date couldn't hurt either one of you."

Grant thought about Cam's words long after they'd hung up. Exterior walls took more time to prep. Applying cleanser to the wall to strip off any excess dirt or oils that might hinder his painting gave him mindless labor to do and plenty of thinking time. Laying on the primer added more time and though people passed by as he worked and some asked questions, most left him to himself. People had gotten used to seeing him working and were keeping back and giving him space. After all, they were too busy enjoying their vacations to get involved with what he was doing. He enjoyed hearing the laughter of children and the moms and dads playing with them in the pool. That was the part of his job that he loved: replacing a boring wall with something beautiful that would enhance the enjoyment of those who would be viewing it. Two days from now, if these families were still visiting at the resort, he hoped his mural would make them laugh and smile in wonderment. And that was the gift his talent gave him. Those smiles and happy faces. But today his mind was lost in thought of only one face: Cali's.

When he was finished with his priming, he gathered up his supplies and cleaned up his tools.

"How's it going?" Cali's sweet voice broke into his musings. He turned to find her just steps away from him. His pulse had jumped at the sound of her voice and it surged when he found her smiling face. "Do you want me to get someone from maintenance to do that for you?"

He placed his hands on his hips and just took her in. "I like to do this myself. That way I know it's right. Besides, Horace already offered."

"I see. As long as you're sure. Look, I have to go to my parents' house for dinner. I completely forgot about it until Jillian mentioned it a few minutes ago. They'd love for you to come too."

He paused. She looked conflicted about asking him. Disappointment washed over him. "You don't look real enthusiastic about the prospect."

She rubbed the crease that formed between her eyes.

Behind her, a child squealed with glee and then jumped from the side of the pool into the water. He saw this out of his peripheral vision because his eyes held Cali's.

"Don't get me wrong. I love my family desperately. But...since my divorce, they..." Her nose wrinkled slightly and he almost smiled. "They hover. They want what's best for me and I almost think..." She paused and shook her head. "Sorry, scratch that. Family events can be suffocating at times, that's all. I want to make them happy and to stop their worry at the same time. But it's exhausting. And that sounds terrible."

He smiled and held back a laugh at her truthfulness. "Go, relax and just enjoy your time with them. They mean well. I know Cam does, if he pushes, and I think he probably does. He didn't talk about you much before I came out here but in the little he told me, I could hear the protectiveness in his voice. Him not telling me about you was, in a way, part of that, I think."

She tucked hair behind her ear. "He's giving me space, but then, he's a long way away from Windswept Bay."

"True." He couldn't take his eyes off her and didn't like seeing her like this. Almost uncertain of herself.

"Come with me. Really. My family would love to meet you. My mom is actually planning on asking you to dinner one night. She's probably planning on discussing that tonight. She just didn't want to interfere with your concentration and your work. All that creativity, you know."

He smiled. He wanted to go. Anything that would get him time with her, he was all in. "Still, it sounds like I might be intruding tonight."

"No, you would be welcomed. And to be honest, I should have already invited you but I worried you wouldn't want to come. I didn't want to take up your time. But, tonight you would take pressure off me. I'm shamelessly using you, not only here at the resort but in this dinner invitation also."

He grinned. "Use me all you want. Sounds like fun."

She swallowed hard. "Yes, sure. So you don't mind?"

"Mind? I just said it sounds like fun. More plainly, I'd love to go with you." *Anywhere, anytime.*

"Great."

"Will all of your family be there? Other than Cam?"

"No. Some of my brothers will but I'm never sure who'll show up at the weekly dinners. It depends on schedules and what's going on in everyone's lives. Shar and Jillian will be there so I'll warn you now. But Olivia is out of town."

"Sounds intriguing. I need to run up and shower. Can you give me a few minutes?"

"Of course. Take your time."

"I don't want to make you late. I'll meet you in the lobby in thirty minutes. Does that work?"

"Perfect. I'll be there."

He fought the urge to touch her and knew he was

doomed to fight that urge all evening.

"Cam has told me a little about your family," Grant said later as they drove down the coastal road toward her parents' home. "There are nine of you. Seven biological and two adopted. Right? And though they don't look like it, Shar and Jillian are part of a set of triplets."

The man smelled of clean, manly soap and his hair was still damp at the edges from the shower he'd had. Cali had been finding it hard to concentrate as she rode beside him in his rustic Jeep. "Yes, that's correct. But we look at Jake and Max as blood. They lost their parents when they were adolescents. We'd all grown up together, so we were already close when tragedy struck their lives. And Shar, Jillian and Olivia are triplets but Jillian and Olivia are identical so they look alike, though age has brought slight differences. Shar is one of a kind."

He laughed. "Oh yeah. I can see that. Your parents sound like amazing people. They raised nine kids."

She laughed because there was such awe in his

voice. "Many more than that if you count the constant stream of friends who traipsed through our home. There it is." She pointed to the house that sat alone on this stretch of the coast and glanced over at him. He was studying the house with deep interest. With an artist's eye, maybe, considering the house was perfect for the setting.

Sitting back from the beach, the waterfront home was a large beach-style home with gray shingles and bright white shutters. "We moved into this home not long after the triplets were born. By that time, we were about to bust out of the smaller home we'd lived in. And later, when the twins joined our family, this place could accommodate us."

"Did Jillian do the landscaping? With the ocean backdrop, it is brilliantly highlighted."

"Mom helped. That's where Jillian gets her talent."

Because of the man beside her, butterflies had been exhausting themselves inside her rib cage as they drove. Now they seemed to have burning wings as he parked the Jeep and the evening drew imminent.

"You're getting off light," she said, trying not to let

her nerves get the better of her. *Would they all start pressing her to date? Would they all see the attraction to Grant that was becoming almost overwhelming?*

"Levi and Jake are my only brothers who are here. At least at the moment. Unless they arrive later, it looks like Levi's twin, Trent, and the youngest brother, Max, are missing. Lucky you. That pulls your number of interrogations down substantially."

"So you think I might survive now?"

"It's possible. Though, Levi is the chief of police. Fair warning."

"I'll survive."

When he said the words, she was mesmerized by the way his lips moved. *Oh boy. The question was, would she?*

Silence stretched between them as she found herself unable to look away from him. Then, his gaze darkened and he leaned toward her... *Was he going to kiss her?*

Butterflies in her chest went wild and her heart thundered at the thought. She didn't move, couldn't. And then he lifted a hand and gently cupped her jaw.

Her breath caught at his touch and she instinctively leaned toward him…anticipation overwhelming.

"It's going to be all right, Cali." His words were a gentle whisper that caught her runaway emotions. His gaze bore into her. "You're tense about tonight. I'm not completely clear why you're so tense with the people you obviously love, but if you need someone to talk to while I'm here, I'm a good listener."

She could not move. His touch was so gentle. Her mouth had gone dry with the want to nuzzle her cheek deeper into his palm. To lean into him and press her lips to his… She jerked upright.

He was offering to let her talk. Just talk.

To listen to her and then leave with all of her secrets.

He was offering her a safe place to pour out everything she couldn't tell anyone else.

Instinctively, she understood that opening up to him could be more dangerous to her than a kiss. She forced herself to pull back. Forced her throat to work, so she could form words. "Thanks, we should go in now. I'm fine," she lied, because she was far from fine and at the moment, it had to do with nothing except wanting Grant Ellington.

CHAPTER THIRTEEN

The initial introductions were made the moment they entered the house. Grant felt himself being sized up by her brothers and dad after handshakes were exchanged. The word protective was foremost in his mind upon meeting them. He wasn't sure whether they, too, were trying to push Cali into the dating scene but they were sure sizing him up.

Levi looked every bit the police chief: suntanned, muscular, with a seriousness about him that probably came from the job.

"You boys can talk in a minute. First come into the

kitchen and let's get you something to drink," Cali's mother, Violet, urged the moment introductions had been made. It was easy to see she was a nurturer as she hustled about the kitchen. She wore her long, thick charcoal-gray hair in a clasp at the nape of her neck and had an engaging smile that dominated her face as she directed it at him with full force. "We're so excited that you're here. I am a huge fan." She reached for a pitcher and he found himself with a glass of lemonade within seconds of her declaration.

Shar and Jillian looked unapologetically gleeful as they greeted him.

Cali had tensed up the moment they'd driven up the driveway; she seemed more relaxed now and yet he could see the strain, like a shadow in her eyes.

As if she waited to see whether her sisters were going to embarrass her. *Did her sisters realize how stressed Cali was?* If they did, they didn't act like it. Maybe being so full of hope, thinking if they pushed her it would help her somehow.

Obviously they could only see what they wanted to see.

He took a step closer to her, feeling protective as he rested a hand at the small of her back. To his surprise, she inched a little closer to him.

Jake picked up his drink and scooped a chip from the large bowl in the center of the table. "So, Shar told us that you have Cali showing you the sights to find inspiration for your paintings. I assume you scuba dive with all that underwater art you do?"

"That's right. I love it."

"Me too. If you need me to show you some places around the island, just let me know. I have a dive shop in town. There's some pretty cool places around here."

"That sounds good. If I can squeeze it in before I leave, I'll do that." And so the night began. He enjoyed meeting the Sinclairs and couldn't imagine getting them all together in one room.

He'd never been around a large family. Not one with nine kids. He wasn't sure what he was expecting but every time he looked at Violet Sinclair, he was in awe. The woman had given birth to seven children. And she'd raised nine. That in itself was noteworthy.

Everyone asked questions about his work, the

places he'd been, the things he'd seen.

Cali's father, Sam, was lean and had the look of a man who enjoyed being outside.

He was a handsome man with a permanent tan and an easy smile.

Levi was tall and muscular and looked strikingly like his father, Sam; Jake was leaner and, because he was adopted, he didn't resemble Sam at all. But it was easy to see he belonged. They all fit. Or what he'd seen so far.

Watching the family made him miss his parents. They lived in London at the moment. His dad's consulting business kept him moving every few years. He hadn't been to see them since the crash and they understood that; they didn't understand him not letting them come see him. He'd tried to explain it to them. It just hadn't felt right to receive comfort from his family when Mike and David's family were grieving. Their families would never be able to embrace them again. The thought sent a wave of sorrow coursing over him. He'd learned that grief came in waves. Waves that could sneak up on him or other times crashing waves that grabbed him and kept him caught in the undertow. Tonight he fought it off, knowing he didn't want to draw attention to himself in that way. His grief was private. It was too close to his heart.

But he hadn't let himself think about his mom and dad's need to see him. Watching Violet as she went around the room, he saw her pat an arm of one of her kids and smooth another one's hair as she passed by. Little touches here and there that showed her love.

He promised himself that he would plan to visit his parents. They deserved to see him and to see for themselves that he was doing okay.

Better now than before.

Cali caught his eye from across the room and she smiled. And in that smile, his mood brightened.

The moon was bright as they drove back to the resort. They'd talked about her family on the way, keeping conversation light while the tension between them was as sharp as a razor's edge.

"Where do you live?" he asked as he parked his

Jeep.

Cali breathed a sigh of relief that they were now back at the resort. He'd taken all the attention at dinner and even her sisters hadn't worked too hard at drawing attention to her. "In a bungalow at the back of the property."

"I don't know why I'm just now asking that."

He tucked his fingers in the pockets of his jeans. Jeans, she noted, that he looked mighty fine in.

"It's no big deal. It's a tiny thing that used to be the groundskeeper's place back before we had surveillance cameras to take that task. I moved in there when I came back and intended to find my own place but haven't taken the time. This is really convenient."

"I'll walk you to your door then."

She leaned back on her heels and glanced in the direction of the beach. It couldn't be seen from the parking lot but the music from the bar and restaurant was playing and the low hum of surf could be heard in the moments between the music.

"Actually, I'd like it if you'd take a walk on the beach with me." She had just officially moved into the deep water.

"I'd like that," he said.

She led the way around the edge of the resort, past the laughter and along the paths where couples walked hand in hand along the moonlit paths. Her heart skittered as she paused at the edge of the sand to remove her sandals. When he slipped his hand into hers, her stomach went bottomless. She'd wanted to hold his hand.

Such a simple thing and yet such a momentous step for her.

Not more than four days ago, she never wanted a man to touch her again. Couldn't believe that she could feel anything for anyone again. And then Grant had shown up.

He smiled sexily. "Can't do a moonlit walk and not hold hands."

"So true," she said. His hand was callused, probably from working on his ranch when he was there. She liked the way her hand felt in his. Though rough, his hands were not hands that would hurt a woman…

He tugged her close; her knees melted and suddenly

she felt tingly all over as he held her. A fierce longing drove through her as she looked up into his solemn eyes. Her breath hitched as his lips covered hers.

And Cali was lost to everything but that moment.

Or found.

Melting against him, she was stunned by the feel of his tender lips and the passion that washed through her as he deepened the kiss. Her heart thundered and crashed harder than the waves off the coast of the island. He dug his fingers into her hair, drew the kiss out until she was breathless against him. And she knew she had never, ever experienced anything like Grant's kiss.

She couldn't think straight. Couldn't catch her breath as he finally drew back, his own breath rasping, "Cali," before he placed a kiss against her temple. And then her cheek. "You are so wonderful." He placed another kiss against her other temple and then her other cheek. And then brushed her lips with his again.

She was breathing hard when he pulled away, and she had to make herself not tug him back for more. Her knees were weak and her heart felt as if it would burst.

"You are so beautiful," he said. "And in the

moonlight you are breathtaking."

It had been a very long time since she'd heard words like his…if she'd ever been so lucky to hear them at all. She didn't want this to end. Didn't want to think about when he would be gone. And he would be gone. He'd said so at her parents' house. She'd heard him talking to her brothers. But for now, she had this moment with him.

When he began trailing heated kisses down her jaw and to the base of her neck, Cali's stomach clenched tightly. She felt as if she were floating on air as those gifted lips blew every hesitancy, every fear out of the water.

All evening she'd watched him patiently answer every question fired his way by her family. He'd seemed to genuinely enjoy every moment of their nosiness and a couple of times, when no one was looking, he winked at her. His antics had played havoc with her, driving her crazy with attraction.

"We better walk," he said after a moment. Taking her hand in his, he led her across the thick, shifting sand to the damp, firmer sand where the tide lapped. And they walked hand in hand with the ocean breeze billowing about them and the waves cresting in the silvery light of the night. It was a magical night. And, just for this moment, she didn't want to think about why she couldn't give her heart away again.

Didn't want to think about why she'd come running back to Windswept Bay, feeling lost and lacking. She didn't want any of her ugly past intruding on the night, though she could feel it crouching at the edges, waiting to pounce. Tonight, she ignored it and held tightly to Grant's hand.

For tonight, she'd let her heart fully feel the emotions being with Grant filled her with. And if she were lucky, she hoped to steal a few more kisses before the clock struck midnight and she pulled herself back behind the walls that she'd constructed around her heart.

CHAPTER FOURTEEN

He hadn't been able to help himself. He'd wanted to hold her all night. Wanted to walk along the shore in the silvery light of the moon. To taste her lips like he'd been longing to do since the first time they'd run into each other beside the elevators.

"I've been wanting this all week." He stopped walking and turned to look at her. "Ever since you barreled into my life at the elevator." He chuckled and she did, too, just before her expression tensed.

"I wasn't expecting this. I think you should know I'm not ready for a relationship. I know that's not important since by the end of next week you'll be gone. But, I need to tell you that."

"I don't have to leave. I've got two murals to finish and then— Cali, that wasn't just a casual kiss." He knew it was true. When he'd arrived at Windswept Bay he'd been lost, floundering, and bleak. Though he was searching for a way to find his footing after the crash, he had only begun and wasn't too hopeful. And then he'd run into Cali and everything had a new outlook. "I know you've been through a lot. And I have a feeling it goes much deeper than you've told anyone. I'm a good listener and I want to help."

She pulled her hand free and moved away from him several steps. The breeze played with the strands of her hair.

Sensing that she needed to talk to someone and wanting that person to be him, he opened his palms. "Talk to me, Cali. I feel like something isn't right. At dinner, it was evident that everyone obviously wants what's best for you. It showed in how they looked at you and in so many other ways, including accepting me, but what stood out to me was your reluctance to let them in."

He was an artist of landscapes and seascapes but he was an artist, and he saw past the exterior and into the interior. Cali was hiding something. Something she needed to release.

"Talk to me. Did your ex hurt you? Physically hurt you?" He hated the words and the thought but his gut told him he was right. Or close.

And he'd never wanted as much in his life to be wrong about something.

But he wasn't. The look on her face told him so.

Grant's questions shot at her tender heart, like darts hitting the bull's-eye.

She closed her eyes and wrapped her arms tightly about her. His kiss had awakened memories that she'd tried to banish. The longing for love. Memories of what she hoped for and what she had and lost.

Irrational anger shot through her. *Why had he gone and messed up a perfect moment? So be it.* "My family just thinks I went through a divorce. A normal, painful divorce from a man who I once loved…or thought I loved. And trusted." She couldn't say this and be still, so she started to walk. Grant moved beside her in quick strides and stopped her with his gentle hand on her arm.

"It was more than that, wasn't it?"

Her chest heaved as she sucked in a hard breath and then nodded. "No one knows."

She'd worked so hard to hide the facts. Just like for the four years of her marriage she'd worked to hide her bruises. A lump formed in her throat.

"How bad did he hurt you?" he asked gruffly.

She felt a tremble start deep inside her body and radiate through her. She clenched her hands, hoping to stop the shaking from taking over. She hated this. Hated it.

She despised being a victim. Never imagined that she would become one. Her throat tightened and she ran the tip of her tongue over dry lips as she measured her words. "I hate this. It started slowly, as the stress of his job increased. Verbally at first and then escalated to the first blow, that was immediately followed by pleas of sorrow and declarations of love." She closed her eyes as memories exploded from their cage in the darkness. *I'm so sorry, baby. I didn't mean to do it. It was just such a stressful day.* Words she'd had compassion for.

Words and lies she'd fallen for.

"He hit you?"

"Yes. And I let him. He begged for forgiveness. Swore it wouldn't happen again…"

"But it did," he growled.

"It did. Over and over again. And I hid the bruises. Like a fool," she muttered. The disgust washed over her. Wished now that she'd kept her mouth shut. Heat rushed her and she spun away from Grant, this beautiful, talented amazing man—who now knew her dirty little secret. *What had she been thinking? What?*

Tears of humiliation stung her eyes and all she wanted was to run and hide. She'd felt like that for so long. And couldn't bear knowing that he knew the truth about her now. She'd failed in so many ways.

"Cali, honey, I'm so sorry." He came up behind her and gently took her in his arms. "Why haven't you told anyone?"

"Because I'm embarrassed, for one. How could I

have let that happen?" She spun and hurried down the beach. Grant was in front of her, barring her way. Through the haze of tears, she could see he was backlit with the romantic moonlight.

"You didn't mess anything up. He did." He tugged her into his arms and held her.

"I stayed. I let him tear me down, tear me apart and I stayed. How could I have done that?"

Like he would know? She didn't even know.

"It's okay," he murmured into her hair, with a tenderness that only made her want to weep.

And she hated crying. "Let me go. I need to go."

"Stay. I'm sorry this happened to you." His hand rubbed her back, kneaded her shoulders.

"I let it happen." The words tore from her even as she fought to hold them back. She'd already said too much.

"It wasn't your fault," he growled, shocking her with the fierce rawness of his words. "Get that out of your mind. He was the one who harmed you. You didn't do that."

"I let it happen." Her throat burned; her head

throbbed.

"No. It just happened." He pressed a gentle kiss to her forehead. "Let it go."

It felt good to have someone to lean on just for a moment, even if she was mortified that he knew. Now she lifted her head. "I need to go. I can't do this."

She stepped away, hating the pity she saw in his eyes.

"Let me walk you back."

"No. I'm fine. I'd like it if you'd forget I told you this." She swiped at her eyes, those maddening tears.

"I want to help."

"No," she said again. The word came out harsh, so she forced her nerves down and said more calmly, "There isn't anything you can do. I just want to forget it. To move on. Rehashing it doesn't change it. I shouldn't have said anything. Good-night." She left him and trudged across the sand as fast as she could go.

"Ignoring it doesn't mean it's gone away," he called after her.

Her head was reeling and her heart hurting as she let the wind carry his words away. She wasn't ready for this. She'd known it.

Right now, she just needed to get away from him. Needed to think. And she couldn't do it with him looking at her with pity in his eyes.

CHAPTER FIFTEEN

"That's looking mighty fine," Horace observed as he leaned on his ladder and studied the mural that Grant had been working on. "My grandkids will love those turtles. The way you have them looking straight at me, like I'm in the water with them and we're studying each other, is amazing. And your seal is looking good too, Jax."

"Thanks," Jax called from where he was painting a playful, yet realistic seal playing underwater.

He'd shown up with enthusiasm about working with Grant, though he'd been uncertain how he could be of help. He'd been surprised when Grant showed him his plans and even more startled when he'd learned they were starting the mural today.

Grant had been pleased to see Jax.

It was going to be a good partnership. One that would boost Jax and let Grant give back and pay it forward.

But Grant had forced every smile he'd smiled today. And every laugh. His mind had been on last night. On Cali and the humiliation she'd felt. It had taken him long into the night before he'd finally grasped what he believed Cali felt.

He'd wanted to break her ex in half. Throw a rope around him, tie that rope to his saddle horn and pay justice the old-fashioned way, dragging him across a rock-strewn pasture full of cactus and briars.

He'd wanted to beat the man to a pulp and if he could find him, there were no guarantees that he wouldn't get the job done sometime in the near future. He knew Cam and probably her other brothers would fight him for the chance.

He should have known Cam didn't know.

Why was she protecting her ex? To keep her brothers from getting in trouble?

The very thought of her suffering at the hands of the man she'd trusted turned his stomach. And he hadn't decided the best way to handle the situation.

He was giving her space and he was doing the only thing he knew to do for her at this moment: paint her murals.

"You look like you're a thousand miles away," Horace said. "You all right?"

"Yeah, I'm fine. I think it's time to call it a day, though. Thanks for helping set up, Horace."

"No problem at all. You boys keep up the good work. My wife's probably got supper ready so I'm heading home. Might bring her by tomorrow to see the progress." He studied Grant with perceptive eyes. Shooting a glance Jax's way and seeing him moving away to clean his brush, he looked at Grant. "I didn't see Cali come by all day. You two have a spat?"

"Didn't you say your wife was waiting?"

Horace's expression said he'd gotten his answer. "She's a good little gal, our Cali. Hurts when she thinks no one is watching. You go easy on her heart. It's a tender, precious thing."

"I know. I'm not planning on hurting her."

"But someone has. So go careful."

Floored, Grant watched the little man in his tan uniform walk away. He saw what no one else had figured out and Grant wondered how.

"Jax, I'm calling it a day."

"Me too," Jax called from where he was cleaning his brushes. "Thanks for this opportunity. I'm proud of that, even if it's not as good as yours." He nodded toward his seal.

"Your work is excellent. Own it, man."

Jax laughed. "Easy for you to say. I painted that mural on the side of the wall just for the heck of it. I never took it seriously. To tell you the truth, this is still freaking me out a little bit that I'm actually painting with you. But, I like it. You're a good guy."

After Jax left, Grant went looking for Cali. He'd given her space all day, but now it was time. He had to make sure she was all right.

Did she plan to hide from this for the rest of her

life? He was trying to understand but he didn't. Why had she stayed? She was a strong woman; he just didn't get it. Never had understood why women stayed in those situations. But he wanted to.

He knew he had to if there was going to be more between them and that was what he wanted. He just hoped she did.

Cali was walking out of the office, where she'd been hiding all day, buried in plans for a wedding, a fifty-year anniversary party, and details for a small mini conference that had just booked for next month.

She was grateful for so much to do today considering avoiding Grant was high on her list and hiding out at home wasn't an option. Shar was busy with the sea turtle hospital today and that kept her away from the resort, a small miracle because Cali wasn't up to her sister's meddling today.

And Shar would have been suspicious if Cali hadn't been down there watching Grant paint. But Cali couldn't be around Grant today, so she was thankful

Shar was not here.

She read the last row of numbers she'd typed into the spreadsheet and realized she'd typed them wrong. Her concentration was shot but like she'd done all day, she erased the numbers and retyped them very carefully.

She wondered how the painting was looking. He'd been at it all day, or so she'd heard. Thoughts of him brought back the vivid remembrance of his kisses last night. Kissing him had been enough to put her into a tailspin but then, unloading all of her sordid past…it was just too much. What had she been thinking?

She hated the way she'd felt trapped in her marriage, hated the way she'd felt afterward too, looking back and asking herself why she hadn't left sooner.

It would have been best to keep it all buried in the past. But no, she'd told Grant.

Jillian came into the office and hurried to her desk. She'd been working in the gardens all day, trying to make certain her crew had everything perfect for next week's wedding.

"How's it going?" Cali asked, pausing her work on

the computer.

"Fine. I just found the most wonderful fountain for the wedding garden. I'm about to head over to look at it in person and arrange for its delivery. Want to come?"

"No, better not. I still have some calls to make."

Jillian leaned against her desk. "Did you have fun last night? Everyone really liked Grant. Mom was charmed."

Who wouldn't be? "I had a good time. He did too. He's intimidated by our big family."

"Ha! Proves we've been right when we tagged him as smart and talented the day he arrived. Have you been by to see the mural?" Jillian asked.

"No, I've been busy here in the office. If he needs me, he knows to call." She hoped that would satisfy Jillian. Questions appeared in her sister's eyes.

"I can't believe you didn't go peek. I just came that way and it's rough at the moment but taking shape. He's also normal and not obsessed like before. He told me this one is shaping up in sections. A gorgeous sea turtle and a seal are pretty much finished and they look fabulous. Jax is really talented."

"I know, he is." Disbelieving and relieved at the same time that she wasn't getting the third degree about not going to see the mural, Cali jumped on Jax and pushed the conversation toward him. "Grant really wants to help him give some support and recognition his way."

"I love that. Okay, I've got to run. I'm supposed to look at the fountain in thirty minutes." She started toward the door and then paused. "You sure you're okay? You seem quiet."

"I'm fine. Please stop worrying about me."

"Okay, okay. Ta-ta for now. See you tomorrow."

And then she was gone. Curiosity burned through Cali. *What did the mural look like?*

She checked her watch. It was almost five, so maybe they had called it a day and he'd gone to his room.

Maybe she could just go down and take a peek. She didn't have to go all the way over to the courtyard to see it. She could stop at the swan bridge and be able to view it just fine.

Before she could talk herself out of it, Cali headed

out of the office and down the back staircase that led out to a private employee entrance that opened into the courtyard beside the swan lagoon.

She walked along the path and over the small bridge. People were everywhere, so that was good—okay, so she felt like a child sneaking around, but her curiosity had her moving forward until she could see the wall. She halted; her hand went to her throat. Even from this distance, she could see the blue background and the seal and turtle. It was going to be outstanding.

"Well, hey there, stranger."

Cali yelped and spun toward Grant. He'd come up behind her and stood there on the swan bridge, looking as good as an ice cream cone on a hot day.

"Didn't mean to startle you."

Her heart thundered and momentarily she wondered why in the world she would even try to hide from this man. "I came to look."

He wasn't smiling. Just looking at her, as if searching for something. Her mind more than likely considering he probably thought she'd lost it last night.

"It's gorgeous." She pulled her gaze from him to

focus on the painting.

"Are you all right? I thought you'd come down earlier."

He moved closer to her and her traitorous body reacted to his nearness as warmth flooded through her. "I had a lot of important work to do."

His expression tensed. "I thought the mural was important. I thought you'd want to make sure I was painting something you approved of."

"And I thought you got your inspiration and painted what you wanted. That was the impression you gave me when you first arrived."

"And you made it clear you had ideas. I'm hoping—" He rubbed his neck, looking away from her momentarily before he cut back to her. "What are we doing, Cali? I don't want to skirt the issues. I'm worried about you. I care about you."

Her heart stumbled and then raced. "I can't do this, Grant. You heard what I went through. I'm not ready for a relationship. I can't—"

"I'm not ready for you to avoid me."

The solid statement and certainty of his words and

voice stopped her denial. They stared at each other, silence and tension straining between them. Cali's heart squeezed tightly and then thundered in her chest.

"I didn't avoid you. I just needed some space after last night."

"I kissed you before I understood what you'd been through. I hope you know that I wouldn't do anything to harm you."

"I want to believe that but can one ever truly know that about someone?"

"It's called trust. And he took that from you. I want to give it back to you. I'd never hurt you. I'm not him." Disgust rang in his words.

"I'm not ready and I don't think I ever will be." The words sounded stale to her ears as her gaze took in every line and contour of Grant's face.

His jaw hardened at her words. "I thought a lot about what you went through and I can see how trusting someone new would be an issue. An understandable issue. But I wouldn't hurt you, Cali."

Her heart clutched. *Did he really understand?* She gave a slight nod.

"Cali, I'm not your ex. Just remember that. Now, how about I show you the painting?"

She nodded. His determination was a definite attraction. "Lead the way."

He smiled. "I plan to."

She was certain he wasn't talking about the painting as he turned and took the lead across the courtyard. She watched him walk away, lean hips and strong back and arms she still remembered the feel of embracing her…and she stepped out and followed him.

CHAPTER SIXTEEN

Two days after he'd started the mural at the pool, it was finished. Grant studied it with a critical eye, as he always did, looking for anything that needed attention. He'd worked hard on it, with Jax beside him.

"I like it." Jax stood beside Grant. "And the kids dig it too."

That was the part Grant loved: watching the kids enjoy his work. They were out of the pool, touching the animals with their fingertips as they oohed and aahed over it. Their parents had all told him and Jax how much they loved it. Many of those who'd watched them begin it were sad to leave before they saw the finished product, but those who'd happened to check in that first day he'd started were able to see the entire process and were enthusiastic about having been there for the entire project.

"Thanks for your help, Jax. You're bringing joy to those kids and many more to come."

"I like the feeling." Satisfaction resonated in his words.

"So you're ready to tackle the exterior wall?"

"Hey, you say jump and I jump. I'm more than ready."

"You sound like me when I got the bug. We'll start in two days. Take the weekend off. I'm sure you have things to tend to at the lagoon."

"I do. And I need to spend some time with my girl. Speaking of, there she is. I'll catch you in two days." He grinned and jogged off to sweep up the young woman Grant had met a few days ago. They looked young and happy as they walked back into the resort.

He wished his and Cali's relationship could be so easy.

As he'd promised, Grant had pulled back and was taking his time. He understood that he had to build trust with Cali if he had any shot at winning her over.

"I like the turtles." Shar came up behind him.

"Thanks. I hear you're very involved in saving turtles."

"I am. I'm on my way there now. We're taking a recovered turtle and releasing it back into the ocean this afternoon, so I'm really excited."

"I was in the Florida Keys last year and just happened to be on the Bahia Honda Beach when the Marathon Key Turtle Hospital came out and released a recovered sea turtle. It was a really inspiring moment. People were everywhere. And when they released it and it swam into the water, everyone cheered."

"Exactly. It is an exciting moment. We rescue the turtles in all kinds of shape—from having infections to digestive tract troubles to having bites taken out of them. All kinds of things happen to these magnificent animals and we doctor them and give them time to get healthy again and then we set them free. It is a celebration in every form of the word." Her face was lit up as she talked. It was easy to see that Cali's sharp-witted sister had a soft spot for creatures of the sea.

"Hey you two." Cali came up, wearing a smile that caused his pulse to quicken just by the flash of it.

She looked at ease today. She'd come by several times over the last couple of days to look at the painting. They'd kept everything about the job and he hadn't pushed, just like he'd said he would. That didn't mean he hadn't wanted to wrap his arms around her and kiss those amazing lips of hers.

"You should come to the release." Shar's expression lit up.

"What?" Cali asked.

"To the turtle release. We're doing it at four, just down the beach. We're releasing Jason Bourne this afternoon. It'll be great. Come to it, Grant, and bring Cali." She winked and started to walk away.

"Hey, wait," he said. "What's this about Jason Bourne? Who is that?"

She laughed. "You know, from the movies about Jason Bourne. It's our turtle. Whoever finds the turtle and calls the 911 number gets to name the turtle. This guy decided to name his rescue after the movie hero that Matt Damon plays. The guy said he hoped to inspire Jason, the turtle Jason, to be stealthy and a fighting machine like the movie character he's named after."

Grant chuckled at the vision of a sea turtle fighting machine. "I just can't picture it but I appreciate his thought." He looked at Cali. "I'd like to go. Do you want to go with me?"

"Cali's already coming," Shar said. "You can show him where the beach is. We need all the support we can get. Come see what our little hospital does and maybe you'll want to get involved in some way."

"What do you say?" he asked Cali.

"Sure. I've got to finish up here and then I'll meet you out front about two. I want to get there early so we can be up front when they release our stealthy turtle back into the wild. I love watching it."

"Will there be a big crowd?"

"Oh yes. We let our guests know about it in case they want to go and the islanders love to cheer the turtles on."

"You'll love it," Shar quipped. "And maybe with

you having painted the turtles on this incredible mural, we'll get some publicity somehow." Shar looked at Cali. "PR pro, can you get us some extra publicity with this?"

"I'll sure give it a whirl. We'll mention it when the paparazzi shows up."

He laughed, liking the joke. "On a serious note, I'd like to donate and I will mention it when I'm interviewed by the magazines we've agreed to be interviewed by. It's the first interviews I've done since the plane crash, so there will be some exposure."

Shar thanked him and then left, not wanting to be late to help.

"Is it going to be hard on you to be interviewed? I'm really grateful you've agreed to this but I hadn't thought about this being the first interviews since the tragedy. Are you okay?"

"I'm better than I was. This is good for me, Cali, so don't feel bad. As much as I feel guilty, I understand that I can't stay stagnant, treading water any longer. Coming here was the right move. Cam knew it too."

"I'm glad." She looked conflicted. "I need to go and then meet you in a few minutes, but why did you listen to Cam?"

"Because I owed him. And he came at it from the angle that I'd be helping his family. That motivated me to at least make a move."

Her expression softened. "Good. I'll see you soon."

She hurried away, hips swaying, and he watched her until she disappeared into one of the buildings. She was going with him in a few minutes and he was going to have to force himself to act casual, as if he wasn't falling in love with her.

Or already had fallen in love with her.

CHAPTER SEVENTEEN

The sun was high on the gorgeous day, with cotton-ball clouds hovering in a gentle blue sky. Cali found herself smiling as she and Grant walked down the sidewalk from the resort toward the Casablanca Restaurant and the beach behind it where Jason Bourne, the sea turtle, would be released into the ocean.

For the last couple of days, she'd worried over spreadsheets and made publicity calls to get the word out about what was going on at the resort. Now that Grant was here and the paintings were happening, it was time to really let the public know so the resort could benefit. And they could really use the publicity as the slow season would be upon them before long and it would really be helpful if more people knew about Windswept Bay. Plus, room renovations were about to begin and that took dollars, not to mention the air conditioner that might crater any day. It was stressful and nerve-racking but with an aging resort, she'd known it came with the territory. Despite all the worry and stress of that, she'd made certain to spend time watching Grant work. The concentration and talented skill that he showed as he and Jax brought his vision to life was addictive, incredibly moving. Watching the people around him respond to what he was creating touched her.

As she'd thought from the beginning, he was exceptional from a distance. And he remained so even after meeting him. He hadn't turned out to be some high-strung talented jerk in person; instead, he'd turned out better than anything she could have imagined.

And she found herself falling for him. And it scared her to death.

It seemed so unrealistic, a product of the romantic

atmosphere of the island and time they'd spent in the moonlight and tropical paradise while he'd searched for inspirations. But, even knowing this didn't stop how she felt when he looked at her…as if she was the only person in the world who mattered.

When she looked into his eyes, so many emotions cascaded through her; when she was near him, every nerve in her body was alive.

Like now. As they walked, their arms brushed; each time it happened, butterflies fluttered and her heart danced.

He'd given her space. He hadn't pressed or pushed for more and he'd let her secrets settle back into the shadows, where she wanted them. At least for now, and she was grateful.

She was fearful of being wrong and of giving up control of her life again; she couldn't help it. She also couldn't deny that she adored him. And she missed his kisses and his arms.

"So, let me get this straight." His words cut into her thoughts. "If I were to see a sea turtle in the bay that appeared hurt and I called the emergency number and they rescued it, I would get to name the turtle I'd helped save?"

"Yes, and that's the reason when you go to the hospital and see all of the turtles the names are very entertaining. For example, the turtle of the hour is Jason Bourne, named from a character in a movie. Others are named for children, girlfriends, ex-girlfriends. Others from traits, like Bubble Rump. He's named this because he has the common bubble butt ailment—hey, don't laugh. It's really a very serious, and common, condition. Someone named him because when they found him he couldn't get his rump to go under water. Thus Bubble Rump because it stuck up out of the water constantly."

"Why? What causes that?"

She frowned. "Digestive problems are one of the most common problems sea turtles suffer from. Their main food is jellyfish. They eat them and help keep the population controlled. But a simple white plastic bag from a grocery store that's floating in the water, having been thrown overboard or from having blown out of someone's boat, looks like a jellyfish to a sea turtle. When they gobble it up, it really causes problems in the intestinal tract. Gas and bloating trapped inside the turtle causes bubble butt. And though it's a kind of amusing name, it's dangerous and a very sad problem for the turtles. They eat other things, too, that cause problems, so their digestive systems are just troublesome."

"What do they do for them?"

"Feed them healthy oils and Maalox and other things to help clean out their digestive tracts and limited diets. Sometimes they have to operate. It takes months at the hospital with careful diets and observation in the pools for them to recover from this."

"Who knew? I knew some about the problems sea turtles face but haven't heard this."

They were nearly to the restaurant, so she left the sidewalk and headed along the path that led around the side and down to the beach. "Shar is really knowledgeable and passionate about the turtles and she's dedicated to helping them. I've learned what I know from her."

"And you're not passionate about it? You sounded as if you care very much."

"Oh, I do. I didn't mean it to sound like I didn't. It's

just for Shar it's a calling. She dedicates endless hours trying to help them."

"So what are you passionate about?"

They walked down the sandy incline toward the area that was roped off, where the turtle ambulance with its turtle lift would soon arrive and they'd lower the turtle to the sand with the special lift. She thought about his question as they trudged through the sand.

"I'd say, since coming back here, I'm passionate about getting our resort back up to being its best. So people can come here and learn about the sea life. I think that's why I relate to your work so much."

She hadn't really given it that much thought but now that he'd brought it up, she knew it was true. *And him.* And that terrified her.

"Why do you look so troubled?" He reached for her hand as they moved up a sand dune. Tingles coursed up her arm as he gently helped her up the hill.

"I'm not—" She found herself standing close to him, looking up into his fathomless blue eyes. "It's nothing."

His gaze flickered to her lips and his head dipped;

her breath caught, thinking he was going to kiss her. And she wanted him to.

"I don't believe you," he murmured instead and stepped away. "Here comes the crowd."

Her mouth was dry as she turned to look toward the people moving across the beach. The orange turtle ambulance appeared. All she could think about was that he'd wanted to kiss her and for that instant, she'd forgotten all of her fears and just wanted that kiss.

Grant stood beside Cali as Shar and the other members of the team lowered the huge sea turtle to the water's edge. They lowered it to the sand from the specially equipped ambulance using a mechanical platform. A crowd had formed on two sides, leaving a wide corridor for the turtle. Everyone watched and cheered as the once very ill sea turtle made his way back out to sea.

"That was amazing," he said, as Jason Bourne swam out and then dove out of sight.

"He's been tagged now and they'll be able to track

him."

"That's great." The ocean breeze lifted her hair and it fluttered around her face. Grant wanted nothing else except to paint her in the moment. He'd decided that he could paint her all the time or scenes with her in them all the time. He never tired of looking at her.

"Do you have time to tour the sea turtle hospital now? I'd love to see it." He did want to see it, but he wanted to spend more time with her and the tour would give him that opportunity. "Say yes," he urged.

"Yes," she answered quickly and he got the impression that she'd shocked herself with her answer.

He would take what he could get. He just didn't want her to shut him out again.

A few minutes later, they arrived at the small, nondescript building. It reminded him a lot of the one in Marathon Key, Florida that he'd seen when he'd been in the Keys: a low-slung building painted a colorful peach and a line of bungalows behind it. He'd been told that the hospital in the Keys was the first of its kind in the world. It had been a motel that the founder had purchased for the saltwater pool that was there. A pool that could hold the recovering turtles prior to their release back into the ocean.

"Was this a motel like the one in Marathon Key?"

"Yes. The founder of this one got the idea from the one there. It also has a saltwater pool. Did you know that one had one?"

"I did. I wanted to tour it but never had the time."

"It's wonderfully interesting. They do short educational lectures when they're open to the public but today I'll have to be your guide."

"All the better."

She laughed. "You say that now, but I don't know all the cool details."

"You'll know enough, I'm sure."

They toured the operating area and the examination rooms. She took him out back; several large above-ground pools had turtles of all sizes and shapes swimming in blue waters: leatherbacks and massive loggerheads and smaller ones too.

He instantly spotted several that had their rears bobbing, making it slightly awkward for the turtles to swim. Each had what looked like small, flat weights the size of half dollars adhered to their shells". "What are those black things on their shells?"

"I'm sure you've guessed but they are the ones suffering from digestive disorders with bloating. Those are weights to help hold their lower half in the water as the meds slowly help their digestive tracts get back to normal. Sadly, many of them with this condition have to stay here forever. You'll see a lot of those, some bigger than others depending on the age of the turtle."

And it was true, he saw, as they moved to more pools and then some smaller pools with sicker turtles that needed to be alone during the healing process.

"I'm assuming that folks who intentionally throw trash in the ocean are not appreciated. It looks like digestive problems are the largest threat here."

"That and tumors caused from pollution breaking down their immune systems. They are curious creatures and trash draws them. You do not want to be caught by Shar throwing something overboard. Or being careless enough to accidently lose trash in the ocean. My little sis will eat you alive."

He could only imagine. "They do a good thing here.

This is where I'd like you to put the money you had set aside for me."

She looked startled. "Really. All of it?"

"Unless you have a better use for it? I'll leave that up to you, but I would like a portion of it here and I'll make a separate donation."

"No, I mean that's great. Shar will be so pleased. They are struggling at the moment and this will help them. It's your money to give."

"Then this is it. Also, I'd rather my name not be mentioned."

"But, why? It's a wonderful thing to do."

"I'm no better than anyone. I just happen to have it to give. Seriously, Cali, stop looking at me like that. You give what you can, I give what I can—it's the same thing."

"Whatever you say." She laughed. "You're going to save a lot of endangered turtles."

"Great. Thanks for bringing me here. I've enjoyed my day. It's helped me relax and I'll be ready to start the outside tomorrow."

And he'd be that much closer to leaving. The

thought did not settle well with Cali as they drove back to the resort.

Could she let him?

CHAPTER EIGHTEEN

Painting the exterior wall was a bigger job than the other two murals combined. Horace's crew had set up the scaffolds, and he and Jax had lined up the paints on makeshift tables that had been set up at ground zero. A large area had been roped off and the weather forecast was good. He expected a small crowd and a couple of reporters and had warned Cali that he might need her to help keep things running smoothly. He always wanted to talk to anyone who might want to, but sometimes there needed to be a little orchestration between his creative moments and mingling. She'd agreed that she needed to be there and he couldn't help enjoying the fact that she'd be hanging out with him for most of the week.

The idea had him humming as he organized the paint and decided on what he would paint. She was on his mind constantly.

He'd known her for less than two weeks and he knew she was the one. He loved her and he wanted her in his life. He wanted to be a part of her life. And if it took him a lifetime, he was determined to show her that a real man didn't hurt a woman. He planned to gain her trust one day at a time for as long as it took.

There was no way he could get on a plane in a few days and fly off without her in his life. Not when he wanted her as his wife. And he did.

He wanted to watch sunsets with her each evening as they walked hand in hand along the beach and he wanted to wake up with her next to him each morning.

His thoughts were full of her as he began painting the background for the mural. When she showed up with coffee and muffins for him and Jax, it took every bit of willpower not to pull her into his arms. But he managed to control the urge and instead took the cup from her, enjoyed the sparks their fingers made when they touched and the flare of awareness in her eyes and then he went to work on the wall. And Cali went to work being the hostess of the gathering onlookers. She helped answer questions from the crowds that gathered to watch and to talk to the few local media reporters who showed up. And she made sure he and Jax had plenty of liquids and food.

He was glad to have her there.

"I love watching you weave magic with that spray gun," she called up to him on the second evening as he climbed down from the top tier. It was near dinner time and most people who'd been curious had dispersed for the day, so they were alone. Even Jax had left to check on his business.

"Then I'll use it all the time." He paused around the eight-foot mark and stared at her, where she waited on the ground. She was so incredibly beautiful and he itched to paint her there on the sand with that look on her face. "You take my breath away, Cali Sinclair." *And I've fallen for you.*

"You've had too much sun."

"No, you're incredible."

Her green eyes clouded. "I don't know what to say to that," she said after a moment.

He climbed a few more feet and then hopped from the metal-framed scaffold and landed in the sand beside her. "There's nothing for you to say. It's just the way you make me feel." He ran a knuckle along her jaw and then landed a quick kiss to the tip of her nose because he couldn't help himself. "Some things just are. And the fact that you make me breathless is one of those things."

"Are you sure it wasn't the climb down that twenty-foot tall scaffold?" she teased, looking pleased that she'd figured out a comeback.

"I'm certain."

He couldn't take his eyes off her. Having had her on his mind every moment of the last few days wasn't helping him pull back from her. It was a beautiful tropical evening and the promise of a spectacular moon was in the air. "Take a walk on the beach with me tonight," he murmured. He almost kissed her and would have if she hadn't sidestepped him and shot him a small smile.

"I can't."

"Or won't? But that's okay—I like a challenge." And he wasn't giving up. "I'm not giving up on us, Cali."

Her eyes went wide and he wondered whether she understood how serious he was. But he decided not to push.

"So what are you going to paint?" She changed the subject. "This background that you've done with the paint gun has me so curious."

"You'll see. Trust me."

Something flickered in her green eyes. Unable to help himself, he leaned toward her and pressed a kiss on her lips. "I promise you, people will want to see it. I better get back to work." He turned to go to the table with paints. It was either that or sweep her into his arms.

"I do trust you," she said, breathless in a way that had his mind completely not on painting. Had him stopping in his tracks and turning back to her slowly.

"I do," she continued, not sounding exactly convincing.

"If you trust me on this, then we're making

progress." Again, unable to stop himself, he took two steps back to her and pulled her easily into his arms and kissed her again. It was a kiss full of self-control and restraint, because he didn't want to scare her off. "And now, if you want me to get this done, I better get back to work."

"Maybe so." She then backed away. "I'm here if you need anything."

Boy, was that a loaded statement. He needed her. In every way imaginable—heart, mind, and soul, he needed her.

For the rest of the afternoon, Cali couldn't stop thinking about what Grant had said. Or his gentle kisses. And what he hadn't said.

He was trying to gain her trust. And she'd told him she did trust him.

As if understanding how hard it had been for her to say the words, he'd said they were making progress. That meant he wasn't giving up on fully gaining her trust.

But he would be gone soon. *How could he gain her trust if he was gone?*

Would he move to Windswept Bay for her? He had a horse ranch. Cam made it to the island maybe two times a year but rarely more than three. Cowboys loved their ranches and as much as Grant traveled, he'd want to be on his ranch when he wasn't painting some exquisite work of art on walls, making people smile.

She sighed as she watched him paint. Loving the way he moved, the way he threw himself into what he was creating. She loved everything about him.

But even if she ever truly gave up her freedom for a man again, she couldn't—wouldn't—leave the island. Her life was here at Windswept Bay.

And his was only here temporarily.

By the next afternoon, things were not so quiet on the beach. If Cali had thought Grant painting on the interior of the building was a draw to crowds, she found it was nothing compared to the interest in the exterior wall.

The third day, it was amazing how the wall began

to come alive. As it did, the crowds began to show up, gathering on the sand to watch. Everyone was intrigued and it showed.

Shar and Jillian came from the office to help answer questions and give their support. They were all interviewed for the local news. Publicity for the resort was good.

Pictures and video and word began to travel across Facebook, Twitter, and other social media sites as onlookers snapped shots of Grant painting. He did look spectacular up on the scaffold, working on near life-sized dolphins that were coming to life as they watched. She loved what she was seeing and couldn't wait for the finished product. Obviously others couldn't either.

Grant and Jax painting was big news. Jax and his Lagoon Adventures were also getting great publicity. And then, mid-afternoon, things started to shift as it seemed the dam broke as people and reporters arrived in droves. Reporters appeared with their vans and satellite feeds and helicopters began to buzz the beach, hovering and getting their shots of Grant and the mural.

One in particular seemed almost determined to get

on the scaffold with Grant.

"This is getting crazy," Shar yelled over the roar of the helicopter. "Where did all these people come from? The parking lot is full and there's starting to be a traffic jam out on the street. These helicopters buzzing around are getting dangerous."

Cali studied the situation. "Word's gotten out. People who are close are coming to the island out of curiosity. Nothing like this has ever really happened here before."

"That's the truth. And look at him work. This is going to be gorgeous. You had a great idea."

Cali felt pride, knowing her sister approved. "Thank you. Hopefully we'll get some calls for reservations to perk up the coming weeks."

"Oh, we are." Jillian came across the sand, just as a gust from a helicopter nearly swept her away and sand blasted them. "If he gets any closer, the sand might mess up the wall!" she yelled.

"What is he thinking?" Cali yelled in alarm. Spinning toward the helicopter, she waved her arms, trying to tell it to get back. She glanced at the top of the scaffold and saw Grant turn toward the chopper. Her heart dropped as she worried that the helicopter blades were dangerously close to him.

He lifted his hands, his paintbrush still in his right hand, and he motioned the reckless pilot back too, just as a wind gust caused the helicopter to bobble badly.

People screamed and began running. The news crews on the ground were now getting footage of the reckless helicopter as it seemed to struggle. Miraculously, the pilot lifted the machine into the sky and flew away. Cali, Shar, and Jillian had been frozen as the dangerous moments unfolded.

"What in the name of thunder is going on here?"

Cali was dizzy with fear and relief as she spun to find Levi. His badge glinted in the afternoon sun and he'd yanked his aviator shades off to glare at her and then at the disappearing helicopter.

"Do you know how disastrous that nearly was?"

Cali shot a relieved glance up at Grant and saw that he was clamoring down the scaffold.

Levi continued his rant. "There is a traffic jam on the street. News vans from all over Florida are crammed out there. I have my men blocking the way into the resort but this is a circus. Why didn't you give me a heads-up it would be like this?" He directed the accusation at Grant as he stalked over, his expression stormy.

Grant ignored Levi. "Are you all right? That helicopter was out of control."

The intensity of his gaze was locked on her. To Cali's surprise, she saw worry and fear for her there in those eyes.

"Are you all right?" he repeated, sounding as if he was barely controlled.

She nodded. "I am."

Before she got the words out, he pulled her into his arms and hugged her. "I had a horrifying few moments up there, worried all of you on the ground were about to be decimated by that reckless—" His words broke off and he turned to Levi; still keeping his arm around her shoulder, he held her close. "Charges or something should be brought against that pilot. There was no sense in that. He could have harmed all these people."

Levi still looked madder than a bull in a rodeo

chute. "Does this happen every time you paint? Is this normal? If so, me and my department should have been alerted to this circus. And believe me, we'll find out who that pilot is."

"It can sometimes get crazy but never like this. I didn't think about it getting out of hand here or I would have said something the other night at dinner."

Suddenly microphones were shoved at Grant and they were surrounded by reporters.

"Mr. Ellington, is it true this is your first marine mural since the plane crash that killed everyone but you?"

"How does it feel to be the only survivor of that crash?"

Questions came in rapid-fire. Cali felt Grant tense beside her. She brought her arm around his waist and squeezed, trying to give him support as a microphone bumped her in the cheek as some female reporter shoved it to get at Grant.

"That's enough," Levi barked, pushing between them and the reporters. "Everyone back up. And that's an order." When no one seemed to listen, he roared, "I said back up. *Now*."

Everyone scurried back a couple of steps. Despite the way her heart was thundering, Cali marveled at her brother. Levi looked fierce and every bit the protector in that moment.

"Now, if you want to ask Mr. Ellington questions, you'll do it in an orderly fashion or I'll run your butts off this island so fast your heads will spin. Is that clear?"

CHAPTER NINETEEN

They hadn't gotten to talk much after the helicopter incident, not with the reporters and then the crowd jumping in with questions too. From the reporters, some questions were intrusive on the pain he'd suffered and the loss and grief he carried. But the crowd, his fans, had asked questions about his painting, about the marine life he loved to paint and she'd witnessed him come to life during those moments. But, she was afraid the questions about the crash had taken its toll; when they were done, he'd gone back to work.

Hours later, he climbed down from the scaffold

where he'd been working on a school of yellowtail fish weaving through the brilliant coral. He gave her a distracted kiss and held his palm against her cheek.

"It's been a long day," he murmured and then he headed to his room for sleep.

Cali wanted to go after him but she didn't. The day, the heat, the intensity of his artistry—all of it together was what had him exhausted and distracted. He needed sleep. He'd be better tomorrow.

She spent a sleepless night sitting outside her bungalow, burrowed in her patio chair as she listened to the surf and thought about her life. And about Grant. And about her life without him when he left.

On Friday, the crowds returned in full force, just as Grant warned they probably would because people would want to see the final product. He'd been right. With luck, by evening it would be done. Levi and his Windswept Bay Police Department made certain order was upheld.

Despite all the chaos going on around them, she watched along with the crowd as Grant and Jax put the finishing details on the amazing, amazing work of art. It took her breath away.

A gorgeous, brilliant reef started on the first floor of the building and rose up along one side, with vibrant-colored fish darting in and out of the colorful coral. Each day, the lower level of the mural had grown with each stroke of his and Jax's paintbrushes. The detail was fascinating. Jax had been as talented as Grant had suspected and he'd worked tirelessly on those sections after Grant had moved up to the next areas. There he'd painted the dolphins, five in all, playful and dear as they dove and swam in the sun-dappled water below the surface. They looked so real it was unbelievable. And it was more than she'd ever envisioned.

He'd already been working when she'd arrived that morning. Unlike last night, he seemed happier and he spent time speaking to anyone who asked him questions. The intensity was gone today, as if now that the end was here he could relax and enjoy his creation as much as everyone watching him.

Cali loved him.

There was a kindness in him, and a passion that she wanted with all of her heart to embrace. She just had to trust herself.

When the last highlight on the mural was done and he signed his name and Jax signed his, the crowd cheered and Cali teared up.

Shar stood beside her and elbowed her in the ribs. "I hope you aren't going to let that man leave without telling him you love him."

Cali sighed. "Is it that obvious?"

Her brash, bold sister laughed. "From the very start, there was something there. I wouldn't have pushed you if there hadn't been."

Jillian had been standing beside Shar and came to place an arm around Cali's waist. "He's a keeper and worth fighting anything you have to overcome to keep him. Don't you think?"

Cali nodded. It was so true. "Wish me luck."

"Ha, you don't need it," Shar hissed. "Go."

Jillian chuckled. "Yes, go."

Cali's stomach was in knots as she moved across the sand toward Grant. He was moving toward her and they met halfway. Before she lost her nerve, she wrapped her arms around him. "I love you, Grant. And

I don't want you to leave but I don't know what to do about it."

He smiled at her and she thought there was nothing that could ever compare—not even his murals—to the depths of his blue eyes.

In one swift motion, he lifted her into his arms and the crowd cheered again.

"I love you, Cali, and I'm not going anywhere. All I needed was your love. We'll work the logistics out after that. But I love your island. When I arrived here, I was in a dark place in my life. I think we were both treading water. We were both just trying to get by. You and your sweet spirit lifted me up, and I hope I've helped you. I'm home here, Cali, with you."

Her heart was full. He was right: she was here, home where she belonged but until he showed up, she was simply going through the motions. He'd brought color back into her life.

And love. "Kiss me again and tell me you love me." She drew his head to hers.

He paused. "You're going to hear how much I love you from this moment on for the rest of your life. I love you, Cali." And then he lowered his head and kissed her breathless.

And it was only the beginning.

Excerpt from

SOMEWHERE WITH YOU

Windswept Bay, Book Two

CHAPTER ONE

Gage Lancaster strode out onto the deck of his rental, a three-story glass-and-wood monstrosity that Kym, his assistant, had rented for him on the spur of the moment. It sat on a semi-secluded beach on the tip of the small island of Windswept Beach. It was the perfect place for him to disappear.

And he'd done just that; having arrived here two days ago, he'd done nothing but hole up inside the house with no phones on, no TV, no Internet. He hadn't even opened the blinds during the day. Other than sitting in the dark on the deck at night and listening to the surf, he had for all intents and purposes gone off the grid.

Now, he rubbed his grizzled jaw, breathed in the sea air and decided it was probably time to start venturing out at least a little. The misty morning shrouded the coastline, making it impossible to see all the way across the bay where the main hub of the island was. He'd go check that out today. Right now, he was going to take advantage of the secluded beach and go for a quick dip in the ocean before his shower.

Going back inside, he cut the tags off a new pair of swim trunks with a knife from the kitchen, put them on and then strode back onto the deck. He pulled his shirt off over his head and dropped it in a lounge chair as he passed by and then he jogged down the steps and across the beach to the water's edge. For a little while, he was free: no phones to answer, no deals to manage, no contracts to sign. At least for a few days, no one other than Kym knew where he was.

And for now that suited him just fine.

He jogged into the surf and dove over a shallow

wave into the blue water. He'd have to go back to real life soon. But not yet.

Not now.

For now, he was here.

He surfaced down the beach and turned to survey the coastline from the water. The exclusive homes on this stretch of shore were built for privacy and weren't easily visible from the water. Something else that suited him. He started to swim toward shore when he spotted a woman jogging toward the beach. She had shoulder-length dark hair that caught in the wind as she jogged. She ran beside a large, slightly humped rock and then dropped to her knees and started doing something. Curious, Gage swam toward shore. His feet had just touched sand when he realized it was a sea turtle that she was on her knees beside. A huge one.

She was struggling frantically with something on the turtle. Gage jogged out of the water; the shallow waves lapped at his legs as he headed toward the woman.

The turtle was tangled in twine and rope and she was struggling to free it.

A jolt of empathy washed over him and he jogged through the remaining waves toward her. "Hey," he called when he was close enough for her to hear him.

She lifted her head and slammed him with angry eyes full of passion and fire. Her gaze raked over him, taking in his dripping appearance. His pulse jolted as those eyes met his and he slowed his pace and then stopped near her.

"Can you believe they just toss this overboard?" she snapped, then went back to work, so preoccupied it felt as though she hadn't really noticed he was there.

"Can I help? He looks like he's in a bad way."

Her head shot back up and those eyes singed his skin with the fire flaming there. "Yes." She stared at him. "It's hurting him and I need a knife. Or something to cut it off," she said, anxiously. "Look at his poor front foot. It'll probably have to be amputated."

Gage cringed at the foot that was so wrapped in the line that it was damaged horribly. "I have a knife." He reached for the pocket of his shorts for the pocketknife he always carried, the one his dad had given him many years ago. Only, he'd changed into the swim trunks, so he didn't have his knife. "Hang on. I'll be right back with a knife."

"Thank you. Hurry."

Gage raced across the sand to the rental, and not worrying whether he was dripping water on the tile, he went inside for a knife. He was running back across the beach in moments but it felt like hours. She was still struggling fruitlessly to remove the tangled mess, stopping to look up and see him jogging the last few feet.

He knelt beside her.

"Thank you." She reached for the knife. "I'll do it." It was clear she was strung tight with her passion to free the turtle and he let her have the knife. She bent over the foot that had line cutting into its skin and looked like a disaster. Gently, she began cutting away the line.

"People don't know the damage they're doing and the sea lives they are destroying when they are neglectful with trash and old lines." Her voice shook with frustration.

He saw that her hands shook too. "Here, let me." He gently covered her hands with his, stopping her movements. Electric shockwaves tore through him as he held her hands; when she lifted her gaze to his, everything in him hummed with the electrical charge.

She breathed in a short, shuddering breath and she nodded. "Okay. Just be careful. Be gentle."

He smiled. "I will be," he assured her. When she relinquished the knife and pulled her hands from his, he started to cut.

Working together, they soon had the line from the turtle and she inspected his wounds. "He's in bad shape. Looks like infection has set in. Poor big Loggerhead. They're protected because they were dying out a few years ago. And look at this poor thing—it's suffering from people's carelessness."

He heard her phone beep and she paused to tug it from her pocket. She read the message. Relief washed over her. "The ambulance is almost here. I can't thank you enough." As if on cue, a siren could be heard in the distance.

"An ambulance for the turtle?"

"Yes. I called them the moment I saw him lying there in trouble. We'll take him to the turtle hospital and they'll give it the care it needs and hopefully it will survive."

An orange ambulance careened over the rise and onto the beach. It moved slowly toward them across the sand. On the side it said, Windswept Bay Sea Turtle Hospital. He'd never seen anything like it. Then again, he'd never spent much time near the beach. He'd been too busy being holed up inside glass-and-steel buildings, making money. Today had been one of the few times that he'd ever swam in the ocean.

But not anymore. Today, he'd helped rescue a sea turtle, a Loggerhead, with a beautiful woman. He pushed the smile away. *Too serious a moment to think about that.*

"Hang in there, buddy," she urged the patient as she patted its shell, which rose a good twenty inches from the ground.

The ambulance wheeled around in a wide circle and backed up toward them. Feeling way out of his element, Gage watched the woman guide the ambulance toward them and then signaled it to halt steps away from them. She acted as if she'd done this before.

Immediately, a man hopped from the driver's seat

and jogged toward them. He wore tan shorts and a faded red T-shirt with the Windswept Bay Sea Turtle Hospital insignia on the front.

"Shar," he said, as if he was well acquainted with the turtle-rescuing beauty. "Wow, you must have been in the right spot at the right time. He looks bad."

"He is, Alex. His front flipper is a mess," she said without preamble.

Another guy had unloaded from the passenger's side. He came around and opened the back doors of the ambulance.

"Man, he's a big one. Probably at least two hundred pounds, maybe two thirty. Let's load him up and get him some attention. Good work, Shar."

"Thanks, John. Glad you and Alex got here fast." Shar looked over at Gage. "Can you help?"

"Yeah, sure. Just tell me what to do."

Lifting a two hundred plus pound sea turtle was a chore even with four of them. But working together, they moved him onto a lift that was attached to the back of the ambulance and then it raised the turtle up and into the ambulance.

When it was loaded up, he was startled when Shar

climbed into the ambulance with the turtle. "Thanks for your help. You were great out there." She shot him a dazzling smile as she lifted her hand in good-bye and then pulled the doors shut.

John and Alex thanked him again and then Gage watched the ambulance drive slowly over the sand. He could see Shar through the window as she focused on the turtle. The ambulance moved up the embankment and then disappeared, sirens blaring.

Gage didn't move. He watched the spot where the ambulance disappeared over the rise and wondered who Shar was.

It hadn't exactly been the opportune moment to ask for her name and phone number…but if she was that closely known by the guys at the hospital, then he knew where to find her.

And he would find her. There was no way he was going to forget her.

More Books by Debra Clopton

Windswept Bay Series

From This Moment On (Book 1)

Somewhere With You (Book 2)

With This Kiss (Book 3)

Forever and For Always (Book 4)

Holding Out For Love (Book 5)

With This Ring (Book 6)

With This Promise (Book 7)

With This Pledge (Book 8)

With This Wish (Book 9)

With This Forever (Book 10)

With This Vow (Book 11)

Check out Debra's Other Series

Cowboys of Dew Drop, Texas

Sunset Bay Romance

Texas Brides & Bachelors

New Horizon Ranch Series

Star Gazer Inn of Corpus Christi Bay

Cowboys of Ransom Creek

Texas Matchmaker Series

About the Author

Debra Clopton is a USA Today bestselling & International bestselling author who has sold over 3.5 million books. She has published over 81 books under her name and her pen name of Hope Moore.

Under both names she writes clean & wholesome and inspirational, small town romances, especially with cowboys but also loves to sweep readers away with romances set on beautiful beaches surrounded by topaz water and romantic sunsets.

Her books now sell worldwide and are regulars on the Bestseller list in the United States and around the world. Debra is a multiple award-winning author, but of all her awards, it is her reader's praise she values most. If she can make someone smile and forget their worries for a few hours (or days when binge reading one of her series) then she's done her job and her heart is happy. She really loves hearing she kept a reader from doing the dishes or sleeping!

A sixth-generation Texan, Debra lives on a ranch in Texas with her husband surrounded by cattle, deer, very busy squirrels and hole digging wild hogs. She enjoys traveling and spending time with her family.

Visit Debra's website and sign up for her newsletter for updates at: www.debraclopton.com

Check out her Facebook at:
www.facebook.com/debra.clopton.5

Follow her on Instagram at: debraclopton_author

or contact her at debraclopton@ymail.com

From This Moment On

Hurt by her failed marriage and dashed dreams, Cali Sinclair returns home to Windswept Bay with her heart wary and closed to the dreams of true love she so desperately wanted. Determined to never again risk her heart, she throws herself into running the family's small boutique resort on the Florida coast, a place so full of romance that it's a reminder every day of what she'll never have. But when renowned artist Grant Ellington shows up to paint a mural on the wall of the resort, she's swept away by her response to the artist. Suddenly, every time he looks at her, Cali finds it harder than she ever thought possible to keep her heart protected.

Grant Ellington loves his ranch, his horses, and his life as a sought-after artist. But after walking away from a plane crash that killed his best friend and the young pilot, he's still struggling with survivor's guilt as he heads to Windswept Bay. Painting a sea life mural at the resort started out as a favor to his neighbor, but one meeting with the beautiful Cali and he feels alive again—and determined to spend time on the moonlit beaches with her in his arms…

But, like him, Cali has her own emotional scars—can they learn to trust the love that sparks between them and move forward from this moment on?